"Do you not understand, Lucinda?"

Lord Sarne dropped on one knee beside her.

"I am asking you to marry me. To be my wife."

Lucinda's lips parted. "I . . . cannot . . . marry you . . . Gabriel." The words came slowly. To her ears they sounded like the tolling of a death knell.

Lord Sarne's black brows drew together. "Cannot? Why?"

Lucinda was silent. Tears were falling from her eyes.

"Don't!" His voice had dropped to a hoarse whisper. "Don't cry, Lucinda!"

For a moment their eyes met and he saw a profound anguish in hers.

"What is it?" he asked anxiously. "Tell me!"

She shook her head.

He tried to take her in his arms, but she tore free and ran to her carriage. He watched until she had vanished from view. She did not turn round once. If she had she would have seen him gazing after her, his eyes revealing a mixture of pain, bewilderment and desire which was tearing him apart.

LUCINDA
BLANCHE CHENIER

Harlequin Books

TORONTO • NEW YORK • LONDON
AMSTERDAM • PARIS • SYDNEY • HAMBURG
STOCKHOLM • ATHENS • TOKYO • MILAN

Published February 1990

ISBN 0-373-31119-2

CHAPTER ONE

LUCINDA EDRINGTON unfolded Zoë Joliffe's letter and read it eagerly. It contained, as she had hoped, all the latest news from Court.

"The Duchess of Kent has given birth to a baby girl."

Across the breakfast table from her, Arthur Edrington groaned.

Lucinda's brown eyes narrowed. "What's the matter, Arthur?"

Her half brother attacked a slice of plum cake with vigour. "Nothing, Lucinda."

Lucinda was not deceived. "What have you been up to *now*, Arthur?"

Guilt suffused his face. A flush spread upward from the tip of his white starched collar. In the light of the morning sun, his blond side-whiskers took on a strawberry tinge. He mumbled a few words about money.

Lucinda leaned across the breakfast table. "Arthur, you have not been betting on the Royal Babies, have you?"

"'Fraid so."

"That is disgusting!"

"But it seemed such a good idea...."

Lucinda drew in her breath. *He has lost!* she deduced.

All Arthur's losses were followed by the words: "But it seemed such a good idea".

"How much did you lose?"

Arthur shrugged helplessly and muttered something indistinct.

"Arthur!"

He grimaced. "Twenty-five thousand pounds on each of them," he confessed. "I guessed the sex of the Duke of Cumberland's child wrongly, too." He dropped a lump of sugar into the tea which Lucinda had just handed him. "I was so sure Kent would produce a boy. He's such a martinet. Such a hard-driving man. He—"

"Arthur, really!" Then the penny dropped. "Do you mean you've lost fifty thousand pounds?"

Miserably, Arthur nodded.

"But you haven't *got* fifty thousand pounds!"

"I, er, well . . ."

Lucinda ran her hands through her cinnamon curls. "You haven't mortgaged your land—have you?"

Arthur's mouth turned down at the corners. "Yes." His voice was scarcely above a whisper.

"Arthur! How could you!"

"I'm sorry, Luce." He slipped unconsciously into the childhood form of her name. "I know I shouldn't have done it. But I thought . . . I thought . . ."

Lucinda bit her lip. The trouble was, he hadn't thought!

His eyes, slightly lighter than her own, were pleading for understanding.

"Yes, I know, Arthur." She reached across the table and patted his hand. "It's all right. We'll come up with something."

Arthur blinked. "We? But you...? Your land...your dowry...I didn't touch..."

Lucinda shook her head. When their father had died, he had left Arthur one half of Bluebell Manor and the other half to Lucinda. "If one of us sinks, the other one does, too."

Arthur considered. "Yes. You're right." And then, wretchedly, "Oh, Luce, I am sorry!"

She smiled wanly at him.

"What are we to do?"

Lucinda wrinkled her retroussé nose. "If only Belle were here. She knows more about finances than the whole of Dorset put together."

"That's it!" Arthur clapped his hands. "We'll invite Belle for lunch. We can explain the problem to her. She's sure to know—" he spread his hands wide "—there's bound to be someone she can send us to, someone who can show us how to raise the money."

"*I* shall invite her," Lucinda decided. "I shall ride to The Limes." It would be quicker on horseback. Besides which, it would save the bother of waiting for the carriage. "I shall take Pearl." The coal-black mare had a sweet temperament, and Lucinda enjoyed riding her.

Lucinda changed from her ivory lace negligée into a snow-white cambric riding dress. The Prussian-blue spencer which she put on over it came down five inches below its fashionably high waist. She chose a

high-crowned hat from which flowed a muslin veil
spotted with Prussian-blue velvet dots.

She was almost halfway along the narrow winding
lanes to The Limes, when Pearl went lame. Lucinda
noticed it immediately. "Whoa girl! Whoa!"

She slipped down from her perch, holding her long,
white skirt carefully in her hand so that it did not drag
in the mud. She walked round the mare and exam-
ined Pearl's hooves. There was, she could see very
well, a stone stuck firmly in the horse's left front hoof.

"Poor thing," sympathized Lucinda. "We'll have
to get that out before we go on together, won't we?"

Pearl's head nodded as if in response.

Lucinda draped her cambric skirt over her left arm,
taking the reins in her right hand. "We'll go to the
Queen's Head. They'll be able to fix you up there."

It was fortunate that the Queen's Head lay not two
minutes' walk away. Its sign, a colourful, but very bad
likeness of Queen Anne, squeaked on unoiled hinges
in the spring breeze; ivy climbed up its red brick walls,
and the sound of ribald laughter came through its
open sash windows.

"Morning, Miss Edrington," the leather-aproned
ostler greeted her.

"Morning, Isaac," replied Lucinda. "Lovely
weather for this time of year, isn't it?"

"It be that, Miss Edrington. Be you a-going to The
Limes?"

"Yes, I am. Pearl's taken lame, though. She has a
stone in her shoe."

"Ah, poor Pearl. I'll fix that for you in a moment." Isaac brought out an instrument like an iron

toothpick. He lifted the hoof Lucinda had indicated, poked around and loosened the stone. "There you are, old girl. Better?"

Pearl blew in his ear.

"You liked that, didn't you?" asked Isaac.

Lucinda laughed. "I think Pearl is very pleased to be free of it."

"I reckon she is."

"I'll let her walk round a bit and then we'll be on our way."

"Right you are, Miss Edrington."

It was then that Lucinda's eyes fell upon the Dennet. It was not that she had never seen a gig before. But this one had crimson wheels, crimson velvet upholstery and a black body with a golden coat of arms emblazoned on it. Not to mention two brightly polished brass lamps, one on either side.

"Whose is that?"

"Well may you ask, Miss Edrington. It belongs to one o' two gentlemen—didn't give their names. None o' us has dared to ask for them, neither. The harness broke back aways, so they came in here wanting us to repair it. Went inside for a drink. They've been inside the better part o' an hour, they have. Keep telling us to hurry. We're doing our best but it's hard work repairing a harness. We don't have tools like what they have in them fancy stables. Not out here."

"I can imagine." Lucinda continued to stare at the Dennet. The conveyance was better suited to the fine streets of London or Bath or Brighton, she reflected, than the rough unpaved roads of Dorset.

"One o' them be staying with the Bushens at Bush Hall," added Isaac.

"Did he say so?"

Isaac shrugged. "Not in so many words. But he hired a horse and asked directions there. So that's where he's bound, I reckon."

"Ah!"

"She seems all right now."

"Good." Lucinda smiled brightly. "I'll be on my way, then."

"Let me give you a hand up," offered Isaac.

"Thank you."

Isaac positioned Pearl by the mounting block in front of Lucinda. As he did so, a pair of dandies emerged from the interior of the Queen's Head.

Lucinda's brown eyes widened.

They both wore tall brown beavers. Their collar points were as sharp as knives. Their cravats were swirls of oyster silk into which their chins practically disappeared. Their coats had tails down to below their knees and severely pinched-in waists.

Over his spurred boots, the dark one wore loose Petersham trousers of a butterscotch colour, which contrasted pleasantly with his olive-green coat. The fair one wore a coat of rich, royal blue and wide, flowing Cossacks, drawn in at the ankle, a fashion Lucinda abhorred.

Both men favoured monocles. The dark one carried his in his right eye, the fair one in his left.

As the fair one mounted his horse, an amused Lucinda glanced down at Isaac. He made a wry face and helped her into the saddle.

All at once, the men seemed aware that they were being watched. They tipped their hats with the arrogance of great lords condescending to notice a humble serving wench.

Lucinda remembered her mother's advice: "When in doubt, flirt." She smiled coquettishly and acknowledged the courtesy with an elegant, decidedly French, turn of her head.

The fair-haired dandy trotted past her in the direction of Bush Hall. The dark one, however, paused and gazed directly at her. It was a penetrating look that was sharp, intense and unnerving.

Lucinda felt as if he had tried to pierce her soul. She trembled. It was over in a second. Then the dark-haired dandy got into his Dennet, whipped up his horse and drove off at a furious pace.

Lucinda found her reticule and slipped half a crown into Isaac's horny hand.

"Thank'ee, Miss Edrington." Isaac touched his cap and grinned at her. "Bless you."

Lucinda urged Pearl onto the road. They proceeded sedately, out of consideration for Pearl's hoof and also because the road was a tricky one. An ancient, high, thorny hedge created a potentially dangerous blind corner. Lucinda never hurried there.

As she approached she heard strange noises coming from the other side of the hedge. When she rounded the corner, she found out why. The dark-haired dandy and his Dennet had parted company. He was sitting in the duck pond. The Dennet was sitting in the thorns.

The dandy was scowling balefully and his horse looked equally miserable.

The cause of the trouble was Old Jedediah and his cartful of chickens. Old Jed was standing there, clad in his smock. He had a long staff in one hand, which he shook threateningly at his adversary. Upon his head, his floppy felt hat, flat as a pancake, seemed to quiver with indignation as its wearer screeched abuse at the dandy, who replied in language quite unfit for the drawing room.

Lucinda's delicate eyebrows arched. She surveyed the dandy. His monocle had dropped from his eye. His exquisitely tailored olive jacket was covered with mud and slime. The fine scent which had wafted toward her at the Queen's Head had been overcome by the odour of stagnant water.

I must not laugh, Lucinda told herself firmly. *I . . . must . . . not . . . laugh.*

"Perhaps," she suggested helpfully, "we could disentangle the horse and put the gig to rights, could we not, Jed?"

Old Jedediah glowered at her and grumbled, "'Tweren't no fault of mine!"

The dandy spluttered with indignation, and Old Jed turned his wrath on him. "You've no right to be careering round our roads! Go back where you belong, you—"

"Jed!" Lucinda's voice carried the right note of authority. Old Jed turned away from his prey, still muttering wrathfully, and set the Dennet to rights.

The gentleman—if indeed that was what he was— started to rise. He was too angry to speak, and his mouth was set in a grim line. His eyes burned like black coals. When he was on his feet, he bowed to Lucinda. Then he reached for his hat and swept it onto his head.

Unfortunately, he was in such an ill temper that he did not look inside it first. Half a bucketful of water cascaded from his head to his feet.

"Oh, dear." Lucinda struggled to control her mirth. She lost. Peal after peal of laughter rang out across the fields.

CHAPTER TWO

BELLEMAINE ANSTRUTHER received Lucinda in the
drawing room of The Limes. Her dark brown hair was
glossy and piled upon her head. Her arm rested languidly on the back of the azure tapestried sofa. A
muslin fichu modestly filled in the décolletage of her
peach-pink sarcenet gown.

"Lucinda, dearest! Do come in! Pray have a chair.
Will you take some sherry with me? A slice of cake?"

"Thank you," said Lucinda. As she perched on the
edge of a gilded chair, her glance caught the flash of
gold-rimmed plates and crystal goblets laid out in
readiness. "Are you expecting someone?"

"As a matter of fact, I am." Bellemaine smiled.
"You'll never guess who."

Lucinda leaned forward eagerly, her face alive with
interest. "Who?"

"Sarne."

"The Earl of Sarne? Is he back?"

Bellemaine nodded.

"And he is coming here? Today? But how did you
manage it?"

Bellemaine preened. "His grandfather knew my
father. The sea makes many friends." She gazed at the
portrait on the wall above her. It had been painted

after Admiral Anstruther's death by an artist who had never known him, but it was said to be a perfect likeness of the old sea dog.

Lucinda's brow furrowed. The return of the long-absent Earl of Sarne would have a considerable effect on people's lives in the district. "Then I shall be brief. I was going to invite you to lunch..."

"Oh!" Bellemaine's face fell. "What a shame! I would have liked to come. But it is quite impossible, you know, since I shall be receiving guests."

"Yes, I understand." Lucinda's finely etched features clouded. "Belle, I wanted to ask you...that is...we...Arthur and I..."

Bellemaine's lashes fluttered. "Yes?"

"We have to raise a large sum of money to pay a debt, and we wondered if you could advise us how to do so."

Bellemaine pursed her lips. "I wish I could advise you, and you know I'll do all I can to help, but it is difficult without knowing the details." She glanced at the golden clock on the mantelpiece. "Financial matters can be so very complicated. I could make a suggestion which might be correct for one person, yet be utterly wrong for another. Do you see? It could take hours, days, even, to find the best solution."

Lucinda studied her manicured hands. "Hmm. Yes." She made an effort to smile. "Well, thank you anyway, Belle." She rose to her feet. "It is time I took my leave of you...."

LUCINDA RODE IN SILENCE until she came to a tiny
brook. At its bank she slipped from Pearl's back and
wept as if her heart would break.

Pearl offered her soft velvet nose for comfort.

Lucinda stroked the horse's muzzle. "Oh Pearl, you
don't know what a mess we're in!"

The only way she could see that they could raise
fifty thousand pounds would be to sell Bluebell
Manor. But it would be like selling half of herself. The
servants would have to be pensioned. The horses
would have to go. And Lucinda did not dare think of
the future once that had happened.

"Pearl!" Her lips quivered. There was absolutely no
possibility of keeping her favourite mare.

Tears trickled down her cheeks. When her father,
Edgar Edrington, had split the estate between herself
and Arthur, he had meant to be scrupulously fair to
both of them. It had never occurred to him that if
Arthur were forced to sell, Lucinda would be, too.

Lucinda brushed the tears from her brown eyes.
Arthur would find a way to put off the sale, she reflected. He would delay. He would borrow. He would
get deeper into debt.

"That must not be!" she said aloud.

Lucinda knelt by the brook and washed her face in
the clear, cool water. She did not realize that she was
no longer alone, until . . .

"Is something the matter?"

Lucinda looked up, startled. She was unaware of the
idyllic picture she presented, with the sun shining
through her light brown hair, making it gleam with
gold and red highlights, with her white dress spread

across the lush green grass and with Pearl standing beside her.

It was he! The dark-haired dandy.

He had changed his clothes. A grey top hat, charcoal coat, tight breeches and Hessians now graced his figure.

"Perhaps I may be of assistance?"

Lucinda stared, as if mesmerized by him.

He was driving a vehicle more acceptable in the country than his Dennet, a cabriolet with a bright yellow hood. Next to him, almost hidden by his muscular frame, was an older woman wearing an embroidered muslin gown and a huge bonnet, overflowing with green feathers.

Remembering her last meeting with the man, Lucinda felt uncomfortable. "No, thank you, *sir*," she said stiffly, instantly regretting her emphasis on "sir."

For his black eyebrows raised and Lucinda saw that once again she had irritated him. She scrambled to her feet and positioned Pearl so that she could mount her unaided.

She was so preoccupied she did not notice that he had left the cabriolet. As she prepared to hoist herself into the saddle, she heard his voice very close behind her.

"Allow me."

Lucinda uttered an exclamation as he lifted her up and placed her in the saddle. Her response was not only caused by the unexpectedness of his action, but by the peculiar sensations which shot through her body. His touch aroused emotions Lucinda had never known she possessed, awakened desires no lady ought to have.

"Forgive me if I startled you," he said in apology. "My name is Sarne."

Lucinda stared at him in horror. Twice in one day she had succeeded in offending the most powerful landowner in Dorset.

"And you are...?" he prompted.

"L-Lucinda E-Edrington," she stammered.

His smile held a hint of triumph, as if he had made a conquest. "May I present my cousin, Miss Nona Fitzjames."

Nona Fitzjames inclined her head.

Lucinda coloured. "We have met, thank you." With an effort she tore her gaze from the earl. "Excuse me. I have b-business to attend to."

He let her go, but his eyes seemed to hold a certain reluctance, which puzzled Lucinda. Why should he be reluctant to let her go?

"SHE COMES FROM a good family," remarked Nona Fitzjames. "However, some of its members are inclined to be...improvident."

Lord Sarne grunted and drove on. Lucinda's withdrawal piqued him. He was not used to women shrinking from him—quite the opposite. Ever since he had come of age, they had thrown themselves at his feet. He had taken the ladies of Lisbon by storm. And Madrid, Paris, Brussels, Vienna...

Lord Sarne therefore had confidence in his attractions. He had had ample proof of his ability to captivate the fair sex. Normally he would have dismissed the incident with a shrug, yet Lucinda's retreat unaccountably disturbed him.

He had seen her only twice before: once at the Queen's Head that morning, and once from the middle of the duck pond. He had been furious then, with Old Jed, with himself, with his horse—and with her.

Unlike Lucinda, he had not seen the humour in it. He had not joined in her laughter. He had, in fact, been filled with rage. For him, it had been the absolute end!

Looking back, though, he had to admit that to an observer the incident might well have been amusing. She had a delightful laugh, he recalled. Wistfully, he wondered if he would ever hear it again.

"WHAT KEPT YOU?" exclaimed Arthur when Lucinda reached Bluebell Manor.

Gently but firmly she pushed him into the library, closed the door behind them and locked it. "I was detained."

"Yes, obviously..." he began. And then, "Where is Belle?"

"Belle was unable to come. She has visitors."

Arthur grimaced.

Lucinda studied him closely. "You did it for her, didn't you?"

Arthur shuffled his foot. "You—you know—I—I love her."

"And you made those bets because you wanted our fortune to match hers?"

"Yes." Arthur reached for the decanter and poured himself a brandy. "I hoped that I could propose to her then...."

Lucinda shook her head.

"It was foolish, I know." He ran his hand along a row of green, leather-bound volumes. Then abruptly he downed the brandy.

Lucinda sat down in a red leather chair. "I've been to Challiss and Mowbray's."

"Why?"

"We must sell Bluebell Manor."

Arthur stared at her.

"I've asked them to put it up at auction."

Arthur's lips parted. "Lucinda, you shouldn't have done that. It's a man's job."

She gave him a sidelong glance.

"Yes. You're right. I would have put it off." He sighed deeply. Then all at once he seized the black, gold-lettered family Bible and put his hand on it. "I call you to witness, Lucinda, that I swear here and now I shall never gamble again."

Lucinda smiled. Apart from their financial worries, she had been deeply concerned about what would happen to Arthur, if he continued to gamble. That this was no longer a possibility, was an enormous relief to her. Knowing he would keep his vow, she said simply, "I'm glad, Arthur," and then swiftly changed the subject. "Mr. Challiss suggested we should have open house for three weeks, to allow people to come and view the property. They'll hold the actual auction at the Queen's Head. It seemed the best place."

Arthur grimaced. "How much do you think we'll get?"

"Mr. Mowbray says seventy-five thousand pounds. He said we should not reckon on more than that."

Arthur made a face.

"Mr. Challiss or Mr. Mowbray will take the prospective buyers round," continued Lucinda. "They are going to give us advance warning when they bring people..."

AT LEAST, that was what Messrs. Challiss and Mowbray had promised. In practice, such promises could not always be kept. Most of the time Lucinda did not mind. The prospective buyers were people unknown to her: strangers requiring only a distant politeness. But one day her heart sank within her when she saw Bellemaine's carriage draw up.

Bellemaine's wide-brimmed bonnet was massed with flowers. As she descended, she gave her hand to the Earl of Sarne.

"Oh, no!" wailed Lucinda.

Arthur looked up sharply from the newspaper he had been reading. "What is it?"

Lucinda pointed.

"Good Lord!" exclaimed Arthur. "They must have brought all their friends and relations!"

At least five other carriages had arrived. Groups of smiling men, women and children emerged, carrying with them an air of expectation—as if they were going to a fair.

"We shall never live this down!" said Lucinda gloomily.

"Oh, yes, we shall!" returned Arthur. "Hebe!"

Lucinda's maid curtseyed. "Yes, Mr. Edrington?" She, too, had seen the arrivals. She straightened her cap and her apron. Her eyes sparkled excitedly at the thought of so many handsome footmen.

"Go upstairs and lock Miss Lucinda's bedroom and my bedroom!"

Hebe's smile vanished at his tone. "Yes, Mr. Edrington." She seized the keys and shot upstairs.

"Thank you, Arthur." Lucinda slipped her hand into her half brother's. He gave it an affectionate squeeze.

Then the doors were flung open and the hordes swept in.

Mr. Challiss approached. "These people have come to, er, view the house for, er, the auction, Mr. Edrington. Please forgive the, er, short notice."

"Yes, of course." Arthur's voice was cool and courteous. "Perhaps you would care to show them round?"

Bellemaine advanced, smiling. Her gaze fastened on Arthur. "Since Lord Sarne is with us, could *you* not do the honours, Arthur?"

Out of the corner of her eye, Lucinda saw the Earl of Sarne stiffen. A slow flush burned in his cheeks.

Arthur was inscrutable. It was a knack he had and Lucinda wished she could emulate him. "Of course. I should be happy to take you round. If you will please come this way...?"

Lucinda knew Lord Sarne was looking at her. She sensed him stalking her. Trembling, she kept her eyes on the floor and her hands folded in front of her, hoping to hide the turmoil within her.

The company swept past, into the white, chintz-hung drawing room, and out again, across the hall, into the dining room—all except the Earl of Sarne. He seemed rooted to the spot.

Lucinda cleared her throat. *Never mind Mama's advice!* she told herself. This was no time for flirting. In another moment she would be trapped, caught in his toils.

"Excuse me." She tried to make good an escape.

Lord Sarne prevented her.

She raised her head.

His black eyes were boring into her brown ones.

"The others have gone," murmured Lucinda.

Lord Sarne did not move.

"You—you will be missed," she stammered.

He took a deep breath. "Please accept my humble apologies."

Lucinda stared at him. "For what?"

"For this—" he gestured "—invasion."

Lucinda offered a tiny shrug. "You need not trouble yourself about that. You were hardly to blame."

"But I was."

"Oh?"

"I brought them here."

"Why?" The question was dragged unwillingly from Lucinda.

"Can't you guess?"

Lucinda coloured and instinctively stepped away from him.

Lord Sarne's brow furrowed. His countenance darkened. She was slipping away from him again. This slender, elegant, elusive creature. In another second she would be out of his grasp.

Why? he wondered. Why couldn't he keep her in his company for more than a few moments?

Lucinda misunderstood the cause of his change of mood. "I am truly sorry," she said, "that I laughed when you...." Her lips twitched. She still could not completely hide her amusement. "When you had that...accident."

"Consider it forgotten." As he towered over her, he reminded her of the leopards in his coat of arms, coiled and ready to spring.

Lucinda peeped at him from under her lashes. She did not feel forgiven. "It was regrettable."

"For Jed, certainly."

She met his gaze. His angry expression frightened her. She wanted to flee, but she found that, somehow, he had maneouvred the two of them into the drawing room.

"Wh-why?" she managed to get out.

"Did you not hear the language Jed used? Do you not think he should be...rebuked?" Lord Sarne's tone was menacing. His black eyes were hard, cold, merciless.

Lucinda had a sudden glimpse of the power this man wielded. She shivered. "Jed is an old man, an eccentric. I'm sure he meant no harm. Could you not forgive him?"

"You make it sound so easy."

"Isn't it?"

He laughed without humour. "Jed and I are old enemies."

"What do you mean?"

"Once, when I was a boy, I pinched an apple from Jed's apple tree. He found me out, and whipped me."

Lucinda smiled beguilingly. "But that was a long time ago. And you were . . . stealing."

"It did not finish there." His muscles were taut with suppressed rage. His voice was soft, dangerous. "He told my father, too. My father beat me so severely that I still bear the scars."

"You were his son. He was angry because he loved you—"

"Loved me! My father? You must be joking! No, Miss Edrington, my father did not love me. He did not love me because he did not love my mother. He made the match in order to produce an heir. My mother came from good stock, you see. She fitted his list of requirements."

Lucinda was silent. Nervously, her fingers plucked at the skirt of her striped lilac gown.

"To my father, my mother was no better than a prize cow," continued the earl. "He was happy to be her stud. Their marriage was a bitter mockery. At first she did not know it. When she finally realized how little he cared for her, it broke her heart. She died. That was when he and I had our great quarrel—and I left."

"Oh." Lucinda bit her lip. "I am sorry. I did not know." She twisted a dainty, lace-edged linen handkerchief in her hands. "But Jed has probably forgotten all about that incident. He's a funny old man...and poor. For him, an apple from his one tree meant much more than it ever could to someone who could afford a whole orchard.''

"So you think I ought to forget it? To let bygones be bygones?''

Lucinda avoided his gaze. "It would be most generous.''

He clicked his tongue. She had backed away, almost into a corner. And that, too, seemed to displease him. "Very well.''

Her lashes fluttered. She sensed the abrupt change in his manner. "You will forgive him?''

"Yes. I'll forgive him...''

Lucinda smiled at him again. Her smile was like sunshine banishing the clouds. Then it slowly disappeared as she saw his face was still hard and unyielding.

"...if you meet my price.''

"Your price?''

"You need not worry. I shall not ask for money. I know you have none.''

"That is most unfair!" Lucinda flared.

"I beg your pardon. I did not intend it as an insult, merely as an observation. My price is in another currency. I demand a payment of one kiss.''

CHAPTER THREE

LUCINDA'S LIPS PARTED in shock. "You—you cannot!" she choked.

The Earl of Sarne's black eyebrows shot up. "Is a kiss so much? Is Jed not worth it? Or do you find me so repellent?"

Lucinda was trembling from head to foot. She felt hot and cold all over. *I have a fever,* she thought. *I am ill!* Yet no fever had ever taken her so suddenly.

Perhaps, she mused, Lord Sarne has driven me to madness. Yes, I am out of my mind! How can I explain it otherwise? No lady in her senses would agree to such a thing!

"Of course . . . I shall . . . pay the price you ask."

She tilted her cheek to him, the way she would have done to Arthur, expecting a brotherly peck.

The Earl of Sarne intended otherwise. His strong arms slipped round her waist, drawing her body swiftly and surely to his. Then his lips pressed against hers.

For half a second Lucinda considered struggling. Then a warm glow spread through her, and she floated on a cloud of bliss. Not wanting this beautiful moment to end, she closed her ears to the sounds outside.

Lord Sarne, however, was more aware than she. Abruptly, he straightened, spun on his heel and walked away from her toward the window.

Instinctively, she realized that he was protecting her by his action. The farther he was from her when the others returned, the less chance there would be of innuendo.

Lord Sarne raised his quizzing glass and surveyed the front garden.

That was his pose when, seconds later, the doors were flung open and Bellemaine burst into the drawing room.

"Oh, there you are!" she exclaimed. "I could not think where you had got to."

Lord Sarne smiled and bowed. "The view here is most pleasant."

His eyes, like polished jet, were on Lucinda. She smiled secretively, savouring the memory of their kiss.

Bellemaine noted the look which passed between them. She guessed that Lord Sarne had not spent the whole of his time in the drawing room ten feet distant from Lucinda, studying the shrubbery. But not a flicker of her eye, nor a quirk of her lips, betrayed her thoughts as she linked her arm with the earl's.

"Lucinda, dearest! Do you know that two of the rooms upstairs are locked? None of us could enter!"

"I am so sorry," responded Lucinda, "but those rooms are private."

"Nonsense! How can anyone form a complete picture of Bluebell Manor if they don't see all the rooms? You must have them opened."

"I . . ." began Lucinda.

Lord Sarne came to her rescue. "I think, Belle," he purred softly, "that one can gain a reasonable impression of Bluebell Manor from what one has seen."

Bellemaine pouted and shrugged. Then she fixed her eyes adoringly on him. "If you say so, Gabriel." She could not hide the triumphant note in her voice. *She* had permission to use Lord Sarne's Christian name. Lucinda did *not*.

"You are quite right, Gabriel." Nona Fitzjames's voice came from the doorway, causing the three to start. "We have seen sufficient to judge."

How long had she been there? wondered Lucinda.

"Aren't you coming?" continued Nona Fitzjames. "The others are already getting into the carriages."

Disappointment crossed Lord Sarne's face—at least so Lucinda imagined. But in a trice his expression altered, and he smiled graciously.

"Then we must not keep them waiting."

He bowed to Lucinda, and with Bellemaine on one arm and Nona Fitzjames on the other, left the drawing room.

Mr. Challiss met them in the hall. A muffled exchange took place.

Then Bellemaine asked, "What would you say Bluebell Manor is worth, Mr. Challiss?"

"We were hoping for about seventy-five thousand pounds from the auction, madam."

ARTHUR HEAVED A SIGH of relief as the last of the carriages departed, and draped his arm over Lucinda's shoulders. "Thank heavens they're gone."

"Indeed," said Lucinda. Peace and quiet at last. What bliss!

The thought was scarcely formed when the door opened and Hebe announced, "Miss Bushens."

Melissa Bushens wore a grass-green riding habit. Her blue eyes gleamed, and blond curls framed her face. "You're in. Wonderful!"

"Good afternoon, Melissa." Arthur bowed. "Is this a social call? Or have you come to view the house?"

Melissa pouted. "I have come to see Lucinda." She removed her lemon-yellow gloves. "May I sit down?"

Lucinda indicated a chair, upholstered in Spitalfields silk with an intricate floral pattern.

"I must talk to you alone, Lucinda," insisted Melissa. "I am sorry, Arthur."

"Of course, Melissa." Then, teasingly, "I know when I'm not wanted."

"I shall swat you if you talk to me like that," warned Melissa.

Arthur laughed. "I shall be in the library if you want me. There are some papers I must go through."

"What papers?" asked Lucinda quickly.

"Boring things. Lists of cattle and seed. Reports on the way the farm is going..."

"The place is doing well. You have a knack for farming, Arthur."

It was an acknowledgment of how the land pertaining to Bluebell Manor had been improved since Arthur had been given a free hand with it.

He smiled his thanks and departed.

"Well, now," said Lucinda to her friend, "what has brought you here in such a state of agitation?"

Melissa heaved a deep sigh. "They're trying to arrange a marriage for me!"

"Your parents?"

"Yes. They have chosen my husband-to-be. Lord Overberry! Vincent, I am to call him."

Lucinda's forehead wrinkled. "Is he by any chance a blond gentleman? Something of a dandy?"

"Yes! How did you know?"

"I saw him with the Earl of Sarne at the Queen's Head a couple of weeks ago."

"Ah!" Melissa sipped the sherry which Lucinda offered her. "'Tis Nona Fitzjames's doing. She has decided to become matchmaker for the whole of Dorset. All fortunes are to be married to titles, and vice versa. Since I have a tidy fortune, I am to be matched to a baron."

"I'm surprised Nona did not aim for an earldom. Lord Sarne, they say, is fancy-free."

"Ah! But Belle's fortune is greater than mine. Therefore our dark-eyed friend rates the earldom. I must be content with a mere barony."

Lucinda laughed. "Wicked girl! But don't you like Lord Overberry?"

Melissa shrugged. "Like? I suppose I do."

"There is nothing the matter with him?"

"No. He is a fine gentleman. A veteran of the Peninsula Campaign. He and Lord Sarne both fought there. He has a promising career in the Horse Guards. He is kind, considerate, loyal."

"A paragon of virtues, no doubt. Has he no failings?"

"None that I could name."

"But there must be a reason you have not accepted him."

"The fault is mine. I don't love him. I like him as a friend. I might even love him as a brother. But not as a husband."

"Surely your parents understand?"

"That's just it. They don't. Nor does Vincent. He cannot see why I have turned down his proposal. He is staying on because he thinks I am shy."

Lucinda choked on her sherry.

Melissa sighed again. "Vincent has concluded that I don't know him well enough. He believes that is why I have refused him."

"Is he so arrogant?"

"Oh, no! He is extremely gallant. He has saved me from the most fearful scolding from Mama and Papa. But, oh Lucinda! I cannot marry Vincent. I cannot!"

"I see that." Lucinda's expression conveyed her sympathy. "But how might I help?"

Melissa looked guilty. "You must support me . . ."

"What have you done?"

"Something dreadful . . ."

"What?"

"I've told my parents—and Vincent—that you and Arthur have invited me here tomorrow night for dinner. I said it was a long-standing engagement, and that I couldn't alter it. Of course my parents insisted that Vincent escort me . . ."

Lucinda's brown eyes widened. "You're not by any chance trying to direct him at me?"

Melissa looked appealingly at her. "Well . . ."

"Melissa, really! I've seen him! I don't find him in the least attractive, and—"

"Oh, but you have not met him. You have not talked to him. You have not got behind—"

"—the monocle, the stiff cravat and those frightful Cossacks! No, you are quite right, I have not. But I cannot take him on. I should laugh myself to death if I had a husband who wore Cossacks. You would not wish such a fate on me, would you, Melissa?"

"Did I ask you to marry him? I only want you to, er, distract him—just enough so that he withdraws his proposal."

"I cannot promise that, either. He may not even like me."

Melissa grimaced.

"But," Lucinda conceded, "you are welcome to come to dinner tomorrow. I shall have a veritable banquet prepared for you to eat. I shall put on my finest dress. I shall make Arthur behave . . ."

Melissa laughed delightedly.

"There!" Lucinda twisted a cinnamon curl around her finger. "If that is any help to you, you have it."

"Thank you!" Melissa kissed her ecstatically on both cheeks. "And now I shall take my leave."

As they walked outside, Lucinda exclaimed, "How dark it has become. Do you think we are in for a storm?"

"I shouldn't wonder."

"In that case you ought not to ride home." Arthur had come onto the front steps where they were waiting for Melissa's horse.

"But I can't stay here!"

"I shall take you home in our carriage."

IT WAS RAINING heavily when Mr. Mowbray appeared later that day, accompanied by Sir Kirby Hookmeadow.

"Welcome to Bluebell Manor." Lucinda extended her hand.

Sir Kirby bowed to kiss it. He handed his hat to Hebe, revealing his greying hair plastered to his head, shining in the light from the candles.

He cast a lecherous glance over Lucinda. "I have come to see the house. I did not come with the crowd, for I loathe crushes."

"Very wise of you," said Lucinda. "Perhaps Mr. Mowbray will take you round."

Sir Kirby Hookmeadow bowed again.

Lucinda watched as the two men mounted the staircase. Mr. Mowbray was stocky, with a thick neck. His form, neither slim nor fat, was hidden by Sir Kirby's corseted belly, the shadow of which projected onto the wall.

Lucinda wrinkled her nose. Mr. Mowbray smelled of leather and parchment. Sir Kirby exuded the odour of oil of juniper and caraway seeds. Lucinda liked Mr. Mowbray. But every time she saw Sir Kirby, she felt she knew why his wife had died: sheer disgust at being married to such a revolting man.

She had once voiced her objections to Sir Kirby to her father. Edgar Edrington had been surprised and perturbed.

"Sir Kirby has done nothing to warrant such violent dislike."

A lecture on judging people by their looks had followed, and Lucinda had felt very guilty. Sir Kirby Hookmeadow had done nothing to her. He had always been scrupulously polite, and yet . . .

Lucinda cringed whenever she saw him. She felt as if his gaze were stripping her naked, as if he had designs upon her body. She was sure his thoughts about her were evil and obscene.

She shuddered. "I shall be glad when he goes!" she murmured.

She selected a book and crossed to the window to sit on the window seat, but found herself unable to read. She looked out at the rain pouring down, and waited for Arthur's return.

Presently the door opened.

"Arthur?"

"No. 'Tis I, my dear."

"Sir Kirby!" Lucinda leapt to her feet. She was alone in the drawing room with him. Her book clutched tightly in her hands, she stammered, "I—I hope you enjoyed the tour of the house."

"It was tolerable," he allowed. "But not as pleasant as it might have been had *you* taken me round."

"I am sorry, but—"

"You need not apologize. A lady should never demean herself by, ahem, selling things." He smiled ingratiatingly and advanced toward her. "I told Mr. Mowbray so before we parted."

Lucinda swallowed. "Mr. Mowbray has gone?"

"Yes. I saw him out myself."

A frisson of fear ran down Lucinda's back. "He will get wet . . . riding."

"He had a carriage. *I* rode." Sir Kirby put some snuff upon his sleeve. He sniffed and sneezed. "I felt it best not to venture out while it was still raining. The dampness—so unhealthy."

"Er, yes. You must remain."

"You are consideration itself." He looked around him. "Your brother is not here?"

Silently, Lucinda cursed herself. Sir Kirby had guessed correctly and it would do no good to deny it. "No. He went out for a drive."

"Indeed?"

"He had business to attend to."

"Aha!" Sir Kirby moved closer still. "I had wished to speak to him. But perhaps you could give him a message?"

"Of course." Anything to keep their conversation impersonal, she thought.

He chose his words with care. "I think it a shame that Bluebell Manor should be sold for want of a paltry few thousand pounds to satisfy the family honour."

Lucinda was puzzled. "Well, there is little else we can do."

Sir Kirby inclined his head. "Ah, but there is. I am prepared to settle your brother's, er, debts."

Lucinda's forehead wrinkled. "You will lend him the money?" she enquired uncertainly.

"No. I shall give it to him."

Lucinda blinked. "That is extremely kind and generous of you, but—"

Sir Kirby smirked. "There are, of course, conditions."

"Yes?"

"First, that Bluebell Manor is withdrawn from auction. Second, that you become my wife."

CHAPTER FOUR

LUCINDA GAPED at Sir Kirby. Horror, shock and disbelief were plainly written on her countenance. "Your w-wife?"

Sir Kirby Hookmeadow rocked on his heels. "I have admired you from afar for many years, Miss Edrington. You have all the accomplishments a man desires in a woman. You would make me the perfect mate."

Lucinda gulped. "I am, of course, honoured . . . by your proposal, Sir Kirby." She paused to take a breath. "But I regret I cannot consent."

"Cannot? Why not?"

Lucinda replaced her book in a gap on the shelf. "I urge you to accept my answer, Sir Kirby."

The knight tilted his head to one side. "Then I shall withdraw my offer to your brother."

Lucinda was silent. She was no longer looking at him. She could not bear to. She had had her fill of his painted face and his damp lips. Her eyes fixed on his boots: large black ones which seemed made for squashing things.

"So, I see how it is," said Sir Kirby. "You have lead too sheltered a life; you cannot conceive of the delights of marriage. Perhaps if I were to demonstrate, you would change your mind."

Before she realized what he meant, he had seized hold of her. His mouth mauled her face as she turned her head every which way to avoid his kisses.

"Let go of me!"

He did not seem to hear her, and she could not escape his painful grasp. Nor could she kick him or tread on his toes. His boots, his damnable boots, were an admirable protection against that.

"Let me go!" she screamed again.

Somehow, she wrenched herself free. She staggered backward, falling against the chintz draperies.

Suddenly, Arthur was standing in the doorway. His whole body was taut, and his face was furious. He said just two words.

"Get out!"

Sir Kirby looked as if he were about to protest. Then Arthur's mouth twisted in a snarl and Sir Kirby thought better of it. He took his hat from Hebe, who had silently appeared, and left the house.

Arthur was shaking with rage. "Please be good enough to ask Yarr to come in here," he requested of Hebe in unnaturally clipped tones.

"Yes, Mr. Edrington." She scurried away like a frightened mouse.

Within moments the butler entered the room.

"Mr. Edrington?" he enquired.

"Yarr," said Arthur, "please would you be good enough to gather the servants in the hall."

"Certainly, sir."

When the servants appeared, they were half-puzzled, half-frightened by Arthur's unexpectedly chilly manner and Lucinda's subdued one.

"I have something to say to all of you," Arthur announced, drawing a deep breath to steady his voice, which still quivered with rage. "Sir Kirby Hookmeadow is not to be admitted to this house again. Not ever. He is not to be permitted to set foot in the grounds of Bluebell Manor so long as they are ours. Whether he is alone or in company he is to be turned away. However influential his companions, or whatever reason he may give for his presence, he is not to be made welcome. I hope I have made myself quite clear?"

Arthur escorted Lucinda back to the drawing room and shut the door behind them with a snap.

Lucinda curled up on the sofa. She had washed her face and her hands, but even so, she still felt contaminated by Sir Kirby Hookmeadow's touch. Carefully she sipped some brandy to restore her shattered nerves.

"Thank you, Arthur." It was a relief to know Sir Kirby would not be calling again.

"Not at all." His face darkened. "I always suspected he was a lecherous monster. But I never thought he would have the effrontery to lay a finger on *you*."

Lucinda brushed away a tear. "He made an offer. He would pay your debts, providing I...married him."

Arthur snorted with disgust. "If I had been here, I would have told him what he could do with his offer!" He poured himself a dram of whisky and downed it in one gulp. "Does that slimy toad think I am going to sell my sister to him?" He laughed bitterly. "We may have to live like beggars, Lucinda, but we'll keep our honour!''

LUCINDA SIGHED as she read the note:

My dearest Lucinda,
    I don't know what to say! It isn't my fault. Really! I pray you forgive me!
    Vincent has unexpectedly gone to stay overnight at Sarne Abbey. So Mama and Papa said that I could not possibly ask him to accompany me to dinner with you tomorrow without also asking Lord Sarne.
    So I did. And the wretched man accepted! I told him that would make the numbers uneven, but he said I was not to worry. He would bring another lady. I suggested that might inconvenience you. He was sure you would not mind.
    I am equally sure you will.
    I throw myself at your feet, Lucinda. I had no idea this was going to happen.

                                    Your ever-contrite
                                    Melissa

Lord Sarne's choice, as it turned out, was Bellemaine. She arrived with the others at Bluebell Manor wearing a bronze turban, plumed with white ostrich feathers, over her dark brown curls. Her dress was bottle-green satin, puffed and ruched at the hem with white silk, bound with copper-coloured thread.

Lucinda moved forward to meet her guests. Her sky-blue muslin dress, shot with silver, shimmered, and her cinnamon curls gleamed in the candlelight.

"Miss Anstruther—" She got no further.

"Oh, please," interrupted Lord Sarne. "Let us be on Christian terms."

Lucinda blinked in astonishment. Every time they met, she reflected, she saw another side to his character.

"Do not be formal on my account," he continued. "You have known each other for so many years. To make yourselves behave with such ceremonious politeness would be a strain. It would be unfair—to Melissa and to Belle. Besides," he added, "we are neighbours. We ought to be friends."

"Gabriel," declared Bellemaine as Arthur kissed her hand, "how very thoughtful of you."

Arthur was smiling broadly. "Welcome to Bluebell Manor, er, Gabriel?" His questioning tone was answered by an affirmative nod from the earl. "I am Arthur. This is my sister Lucinda. Belle, you already know. And you are...?" he asked, turning to the young blond dandy at Melissa's side.

"Vincent," replied Lord Overberry.

Lucinda saw that he was, thank heavens, not wearing Cossacks. Like the other men, he had a tight-fitting raven-black coat, a white shirt, waistcoat, breeches and stockings.

"And of course," concluded Arthur, "you know Melissa."

"I am so glad we are all going to be friends!" Melissa's pink gown swirled around her as she favoured each of the men with an adoring glance.

"Shall we go in to dinner?" invited Lucinda.

THEY HAD SCARCELY touched the first mouthful of soup, when Melissa said, "Whatever brought you back to Dorset, Gabriel?"

The Earl of Sarne glanced up, startled. "I beg your pardon?"

Arthur smiled. "You are something of a mystery in these parts. Nobody has seen hide nor hair of you for ten years. You disappeared quite suddenly, like magic. And as suddenly you have reappeared."

Lord Sarne's eyes twinkled. "I assure you it was not due to any witchcraft or wizardry. The truth is much more mundane. I had a quarrel with my father and I went off to the Peninsula to fight."

"And when the war ended?" persisted Melissa. "Why did you not return then?"

"I was sent to America."

"America!" squeaked Bellemaine.

"Yes. There were several political and diplomatic matters to be settled, not the least of which was the repatriation of prisoners of war."

"And that took four years?"

"No." He sounded displeased. "I also went to Austria and to Italy upon official business."

"What kind of official business?"

"I am not at liberty to say." His mouth closed in a firm line.

"Some turbot?" suggested Lucinda. "Or would you prefer jellied eel?"

Lord Sarne shuddered at the grey, snakelike fish in front of him. "Turbot, thank you." As it was put on his plate, he asked, "Have you lived here all your lives?"

"Yes," answered Arthur. "Lucinda and I both grew up at Bluebell Manor."

"I was born and bred at Bush Hall." Melissa favoured Lord Sarne with a charming smile. "We are old established families. Belle is the only newcomer. She moved here four years ago and bought The Limes."

"Indeed!" exclaimed Lord Sarne. "I thought you were a long-established resident, too."

Bellemaine beamed at him. "Well, actually, no. I was born in Saint James's Palace."

"Indeed." Lord Overberry was impressed. "There are not many who could make that claim."

Bellemaine simpered. "No, there are not." She paused to sip some white wine. "I grew up near Plymouth. We lived there in my father's day. He was Admiral Anstruther. He knew your grandfather, Gabriel."

"Really?" Lord Sarne's forehead wrinkled in a puzzled frown, as if the name were not familiar. "I never knew my grandfather. He died before I was born."

"What a pity," commiserated Bellemaine. "My father married very late. He told me of the American War, when your poor grandfather lost his life."

"I see." His puzzled frown had not gone.

"My father spoke often of your grandfather, and very kindly, too. I said so to Nona one day. She told me she had heard you were returning and she promised to introduce us. As you see, she has kept her word."

Lord Sarne nodded, but his black eyes were wary. "She never mentioned your father."

"Oh, she would not. She left it to me to tell you at a suitable moment."

"Ah!" Lord Sarne played absently with the gold signet ring on his fourth finger. "What's the matter, Vincent?"

Lord Overberry was gazing earnestly at his friend. "Forgive me, Gabriel, but I find it strange that with your houses in such close proximity, you should have grown up not knowing anyone here."

Lord Sarne laughed. "There you see the difference between us, Vincent. You had a normal, happy childhood. Mine was governed by the whims and eccentricities of the sixth Earl of Sarne."

"Then that explains everything."

Lord Sarne responded with a wry grimace. "As soon as I was able to walk, my father packed me off to school. When I came home for the holidays I was absolutely forbidden to play with any of the local children. If Mother had not kindly invited my school friends to Sarne Abbey, I would have been entirely on my own."

"What a strange man!" Bellemaine exclaimed. "So very unlike your grandfather. Now *he* would have..."

Lucinda listened with only half an ear. Since the footmen had been dismissed, she was watching anxiously to see that her guests had enough to eat.

She was also watching Lord Sarne. She had not intended to, but she could not help herself. Her brown eyes kept straying to him.

How very black his hair was, she noted. It shone like a raven's wing in the candlelight. He must have spent a great deal of time in the sun, she reflected, for his skin had acquired a deep tan, making him look more Spanish than English. He was something of an athlete, she guessed. His shoulders were broad, and his well-cut suit could not conceal his fine muscles.

"Bellemaine," remarked Lord Overberry as the bread sauce was being passed. "An unusual name."

Bellemaine fluttered her lashes at him. "It has been used by my family since Norman times, I believe. It means beautiful hand. We Anstruthers have long been noted for our exquisite hands." She displayed her own, which were duly admired.

From there the conversation meandered until it reached Lord Overberry's recent visit to Sarne Abbey.

"Had you been to Sarne Abbey before, Vincent?" enquired Lucinda.

"No, I had not," he replied.

"What is it like? Do tell us!" pleaded Melissa.

"It is an elegant place . . ." began Lord Overberry.

Lord Sarne broke in. "You are being too tactful!"

Lord Overberry laughed. "All right! It's big, rambling, cold and imposing."

"Rather like my father, the late earl. If it's any comfort to you, Vincent, I shall probably redecorate it from top to bottom."

"That would give considerable employment to the local people," observed Arthur. "They could do with it. Times are hard."

"Harrmph!" snorted Bellemaine. "If one is lazy, times are always hard."

"The poor people of whom I am speaking are not lazy. Jobs have become scarce, and wages have fallen. They are struggling to make ends meet."

Bellemaine's shoulders lifted. "I daresay you are right." She smiled dazzlingly at the others.

Lucinda regarded her curiously.

Didn't Belle know? Wasn't she aware how wages had fallen and prices risen? she wondered. She shook her head, making her cinnamon curls dance and cast shadows over her delicate features. Belle spoke without thinking, she told herself, to excuse her friend. She didn't mean it the way it sounded.

"When do you intend to embark on this great redecorating scheme, Gabriel?" queried Lord Overberry.

"When I marry," answered Lord Sarne.

Bellemaine, Melissa and Lucinda choked simultaneously.

"Marry?" gasped Lord Overberry. "You?"

"You seem surprised," murmured the earl.

"Surprised?" spluttered Lord Overberry. "I'm flabbergasted!"

"It is a fairly common estate amongst men and women—marriage."

"But for you—" Lord Overberry was dumbfounded "—you're a confirmed bachelor!"

"Hardly that." He held out his glass to Arthur for more wine. "Didn't I mention my intention before?"

"No, you did not. When did you decide to marry?"

"When I saw Sarne Abbey." There was a strange gleam in his black eyes. "It needs a woman's touch." He raised his glass, and saluted the ladies.

CHAPTER FIVE

BELLEMAINE SKILFULLY DREW the discussion away from the strawberries and cream, the red-currant tarts, the pickled crab, the duck and the custard pie which were being served, and back to Sarne Abbey, and the changes to be made there.

Her comments were knowledgeable, which aroused Lucinda's curiosity.

"Have you been there, then?" she asked finally.

"Indeed yes," answered Bellemaine. "Several times."

"Belle is a frequent caller," remarked Lord Sarne.

"I wish I could see Sarne Abbey!" breathed Melissa.

"Your wish is my command," returned Lord Sarne. "I invite you all to my Midsummer Night's Ball."

"Wonderful!" exclaimed Melissa. "I would love to come! You will take me, won't you, Vincent? Mama and Papa are sure to let me go if you say yes."

"Yes." Lord Overberry acquiesced with a smile.

"You are reinstating the Midsummer Night's Ball?" asked Arthur.

"Yes. It is to be a masquerade as it was in my grandfather's day," replied Lord Sarne, "and to last from seven at night until seven the next morning. You will come, won't you?''

Arthur glanced at his sister. She nodded imperceptibly. "We should be delighted—" he began.

"—if they are still here," completed Bellemaine.

"Is there any reason why they should not be?" enquired Lord Overberry.

"Have you not heard?" countered Bellemaine. "Bluebell Manor is to be auctioned. And that upon the twenty-first of June."

"Er, yes," responded Arthur awkwardly. "It would depend on how the auction goes if I am right in supposing you will hold the Midsummer Night's Ball on June twenty-fourth, according to the new calendar, and not on July fourth, according to the old?"

"Definitely." Lord Sarne was smiling. "The fourth, I believe, falls on a Sunday this year. I do not think our revels would go down well with the Church!"

The rest of dinner was taken up with debating what costumes they ought to wear.

At last the table was cleared. The gentlemen remained in the dining room to drink their port. The ladies retired to the drawing room for coffee and bonbons.

"My congratulations, Melissa," said Bellemaine.

"I beg your pardon?" Melissa was innocence personified.

"Upon your engagement to Vincent. He is a fine fellow. You are a lucky girl."

"I am not engaged to Vincent!"

"Not? But I heard—"

Lucinda intervened. "You must have heard incorrectly. Vincent did indeed propose to Melissa, but she turned him down."

"Foolish child," scolded Bellemaine. "You will not find another like him."

"Oh, I don't know," returned Melissa dreamily. "There is Gabriel."

Bellemaine looked as if she had just swallowed a tablespoon of vinegar. "Gabriel is not a good choice...for you."

"Why not for me?"

Bellemaine leaned back in her armchair. "I hardly know how to tell you."

"You may be quite blunt. I shan't mind."

"It is simply that you could not manage a man like Gabriel, Melissa. He needs a special sort of woman."

"Such as yourself, perhaps?"

"How astonishing that you should say that! Isn't it extraordinary, Lucinda?"

Lucinda smiled mischievously. "Indeed, most extraordinary."

Melissa frowned.

"I do believe," continued Bellemaine, "that you must have second sight, Melissa. How could you know, otherwise?"

"Know? Know what?"

"Why, that only the other day Nona Fitzjames commented that Gabriel and I were destined for each other."

"Bah!" Melissa tossed her head. "Nona Fitzjames said Vincent and I were destined for each other, and we're certainly not!"

Bellemaine sighed despairingly.

It was at that moment the gentlemen walked in.

"Arthur tells us you have a maze," said Lord Overberry. "A real labyrinth, better than the one at Hampton Court."

Lucinda spread her fan and beckoned with it, encouragingly. "Yes, we have a maze. And we are fond of it. It does not get as trampled as the poor thing at Hampton Court, which may account for its being bushier."

"And bigger," added Melissa.

"You must show it to us!" insisted Lord Overberry.

"What? Now?" enquired Arthur.

"Why not?"

"It's dark!"

"You could have it lit."

The maze was at the rear of the house, hidden by the spray from a crescent of fountains. The night was chilly. The ladies borrowed Lucinda's shawls. The men, however, seemed not to notice the drop in temperature.

At the entrance to the maze, Arthur paused. "I suggest we go in threes. Then we shall be able to find our way..."

"That would be very dull," responded Lord Overberry. "The whole point of a maze is to get lost in it. I suggest we draw lots and enter one by one. We must run into the maze, not walk or dawdle, so that we are out of sight before the next person enters."

"Oh, yes!" Melissa clapped her hands ecstatically. "That sounds much more fun!"

"But," protested Arthur, "the maze is complicated. You could—"

"Don't be such a stick-in-the-mud, Arthur. Vincent is right. Getting lost is the whole point."

"How shall we draw lots?" enquired Lucinda.

Lord Sarne smiled. "If I know Vincent, he already has a system."

"So I have." Lord Overberry brought his hat from behind his back. "I have slips of paper folded and marked with numbers from one to ten. Whoever picks the highest goes first. Then the others in order..."

Of course, Lucinda thought, it had to be she who went first. She ran into the maze, guided by the lanterns which Yarr had ordered the footmen to hang.

As she turned this way and that, avoiding the pitfalls and the blind alleys, she heard the shrieks and shouts of the others, who followed. The cries of the gentlemen, the anguished squeals of the ladies as they tried to meet and could not because of the wall of green between them, reached her.

Lucinda smiled. She knew the maze well, better than anyone. She knew she was not far from the exit. She could have left the labyrinth if she had wished but she decided not to. Instead, she slipped into a recess and sank onto the secluded seat.

All at once she heard footsteps. Her head jerked up. The footsteps were coming closer. They sounded menacing as they crunched on the gravel. Lucinda whipped her gown out of the way and tried to hide in the shelter of the verdant alcove.

Lord Sarne was standing in front of her. "I have lost my way."

Lucinda started like a doe in the forest, then her eyes fixed on him. "I . . . I shall take you out."

Lord Sarne offered her his arm. She placed her hand upon it. Strange sensations shot through her and she had to force herself to go on speaking. "The maze," she said, "looks difficult at first, but it is really quite easy once you get the hang of it."

"I am no good in mazes. I need a guide." His mouth quirked. "Preferably a beautiful one—as I have now."

Lucinda glanced sharply at him. His expression was unfathomable. "You flatter me."

"No. I assure you I do not."

"Melissa is beautiful."

"In the classical sense, yes. But I find you more so." He looked at her to judge the impact of his words. She refused to return his gaze. He sighed wistfully.

"And Belle?"

"Belle is a handsome woman," he allowed.

"But not beautiful?"

"I don't know how to answer you."

"A simple yes or no would do."

"I find myself in a quandary."

Lucinda blinked. "What is it?"

"If I say Belle is beautiful, you will call me a liar. You will say that her mouth is too small, or that her eyes are set too close. On the other hand, if I say she is not, you will call me a cad, for a gentleman should never say a lady is not beautiful. It is a churlish, oafish, wicked thing to do. I might even, if such a remark reached Lady Jersey's ears, be refused admittance to Almack's."

Lucinda stiffened. Of course, Lord Sarne had been to Almack's—the most exclusive, the most respectable club in London.

Who with? a small voice inside her asked.

Lucinda made herself smile. "You are quite right. It would be folly indeed to commit yourself."

His black eyes were fastened upon her. He watched her every gesture, seeming to note each subtle change of mood which passed over her delicate features.

"Will you come to the Midsummer Night's Ball?"

She shrugged, unconsciously imitating her mother's Gallic movements. "It depends on the auction."

"And if it did not depend upon the auction?"

Her head lifted, and her brown eyes held his black ones. "But it *will* depend on the auction." Her whole future depended on the auction. "If the new owner wishes to take immediate possession..."

He clicked his tongue exasperatedly. "You must come, regardless."

"I ... I may not be able to."

He wheeled her round to face him. His grip on her shoulders was almost painful. *"You must come."*

The intensity in his voice sent shock waves through her. Why, she wondered, is it so important to him?

"Promise me you'll come," he insisted. "Promise me, Lucinda."

CHAPTER SIX

"How does one find one's way out of this deuced labyrinth!" Lord Overberry's voice was loud in the quiet of the night.

Lucinda uttered an astonished gasp.

Lord Overberry caught sight of her. "Lucinda! Thank heaven! You must know the way out!"

"Yes, I do." Lucinda, still dazed, had to force the words out.

"Excellent. Shall we go?"

"What? Had enough already?" Lord Sarne murmured languidly.

"Good Lord! Gabriel!" exclaimed his friend. "Are you stuck here, too?"

"I'm afraid so," replied the earl. "Lucinda was just showing me where the exit is."

"Splendid. We can leave at once."

"Oh, you can't possibly do that," teased the earl.

"Eh?"

"You must surely be yearning to go through the maze again! After all, you have such a burning desire—"

"Stop it, Gabriel!" Lord Overberry turned in mock exasperation to Lucinda. "He always does this to me. I have a passion for mazes. Most I have seen are too small and too simple to satisfy me. But this one—it must have been designed by Daedalus! Its intricacy has truly defeated me.''

Lucinda laughed. ''I'm glad it meets with your approval.''

''Rather!''

''By the way, have you seen Melissa?'' asked Lord Sarne.

''No. She is not lost, I hope?'' Lord Overberry was concerned.

''She can't be,'' responded Lucinda. ''She would have shouted for help.'' She was walking ahead of the others, surefootedly making for the turnstile which marked the exit. When she saw it, she called out, ''Anyone there?''

''Oh, there you are,'' Melissa answered. ''We've been wondering where you had got to. Arthur said you were sure to find Vincent and Gabriel, Lucinda. But Belle was getting worried. Now, come out, and let us get back to the house. I am chilled to the bone!''

A PILE OF THANK-YOU LETTERS had arrived from Lucinda's guests. Their tone indicated that the evening had been even more successful than she had dared to hope. She was about to take them to the library to Arthur, when she heard his voice raised in anger.

Lucinda knocked upon the library door.

''Come in!'' barked Arthur.

Lucinda slipped into the room. ''What is going on?''

Arthur sighed and flung himself back into his favourite armchair. "You tell her, Yarr."

The butler cleared his throat. "The printers, Miss Edrington, have mistaken the date for the auction. They have put the twenty-eighth on the notices announcing it, instead of the twenty-first. I took the liberty of consulting Messrs. Challiss and Mowbray. They advised that since the date is already on the notices, it would be best to leave it as it is and hold the auction a week later than originally planned."

"I don't see how the printers could have been so incompetent," complained Arthur.

Lucinda stared at him in silence. She seemed to hear Lord Sarne saying, *Will you come to the Midsummer Night's Ball? . . . You must.*

Was this somehow the earl's doing? she wondered. Had he contrived to make the printers change the date? *Promise me you'll come, Lucinda.*

Why was he so insistent?

"What's the matter with you, Lucinda?" asked Arthur.

"I...oh, it's nothing." Lucinda fought to get a grip on herself. "I'm sure Messrs. Challiss and Mowbray are quite right. We should leave the announcement as it is. If we change it, it will only confuse people. It is unfortunate, but it does not really hurt us—and I am sure Yarr has done his best."

Yarr bowed. "Thank you, Miss Edrington."

Arthur sighed. "Yes. Yes, of course you have done your best, Yarr."

Yarr bowed once more.

"I am sorry I shouted at you. It's just that I had it so settled in my mind that the auction would be held on the twenty-first. To endure another week of clod-hoppers trundling through our house..."

"I hardly think that is the way to refer to some of the finest families in the county, Arthur," rebuked Lucinda.

LUCINDA'S COSTUME for the Midsummer Night's Ball at Sarne Abbey occupied a good part of her time over the next fortnight. She had discovered some gossamer silk, the colour of ripe raspberries, in an oak chest in the attic.

It was perfect, she thought. There was no need to buy any other fabric.

She worked on it with Hebe and the other maids for several days. The needles constantly pricked her fingers, and it was a relief to take a break.

She came downstairs one morning, having finished her stint, at the precise moment that Yarr opened the front door to admit someone she'd truly not expected.

"Fernand!" she cried.

He was as tall, graceful and elegant as ever. Lucinda rushed toward him and flung herself into his arms. "My dear Fernand! How good it is to see you!"

"Ma chère soeur!" Fernand was full of Gallic charm. Even as he embraced his half sister, his eyes managed to flirt with the two maidservants who stood nearby.

"Oh, let me get Arthur!" exclaimed Lucinda. "Please go into the drawing room and wait for us."

She ran into the library. "Arthur! Arthur! Come quickly!" She dragged him into the drawing room. "You'll never guess who has turned up!"

"Fernand!" cried Arthur, wrapping him in a bear hug. "What in heaven's name has blown you our way?"

Fernand embraced his stepbrother. "A letter from Zoë Joliffe, saying something about debts and selling Bluebell Manor."

Lucinda and Arthur exchanged glances.

Fernand released a long-suffering sigh. "I was afraid it was true. But why sell Bluebell Manor? Why not come to me for help?"

Arthur shuffled his feet and shrugged, while Lucinda cast her eyes down to the creamy carpet.

Fernand snorted. "You are a proper pair. So very stoical, so very British. Don't I have a right to share in your troubles? Am I not your brother, too?"

"Of course you are, Fernand," cried Lucinda.

"But you have a family—" began Arthur.

"Yes! And you two are a part of it!" declared Fernand. "Now how big is this debt?"

"I lost fifty thousand pounds in a wager." Arthur's voice was hardly above a whisper.

Fernand whistled softly. It was too soon after the war for his estates at Château Niverne to support such a loss. "I must say, when you ruin yourself, you do it in style."

Arthur laughed mirthlessly. "Don't I, though!" He paused and added regretfully, "Well, it's done now, and Bluebell Manor falls under the auctioneer's hammer—"

"And then?" interrupted Fernand impatiently. "What then? What will you do? Where will you go?"

There was silence.

"You must stay with me. You must come to Château Niverne."

"We couldn't!" Arthur protested.

"You are very kind, but—" Lucinda, too, began to reject Ferdnand's tempting offer.

Fernand cut them short. "Nonsense! Of course you shall come. I insist!"

"It's not possible," Arthur tried.

"Why not? Wouldn't you have done the same for me?"

"Well, of course, but—"

"There you are, you see?" Fernand poked Arthur in the chest with his long, delicate fingers. "Enough of this! You will come to stay at Château Niverne! You agree? Yes?"

Arthur hesitated.

"Come, come." Fernand was exasperated. "We have suckled at the same breast. We have shared our childhood. You can't now cut me out of your lives. That is the way to start a family feud!"

"Heaven forbid!" cried Lucinda. "We accept. We really do, Fernand."

"Oh, yes," Arthur chimed in. "Anything to avoid a family feud!"

Fernand laughed. "*Bien*. It is settled, then. I shall write to Dominique...."

"Write to Dominique?" demanded Lucinda. "Didn't you bring your wife with you?"

"No. She is in France."

"Shame on you," scolded Arthur. "You know we would love to see her."

Fernand shrugged. "So you shall, when you come to Château Niverne. But now she cannot travel. She is *enceinte*."

"You are going to have a child?"

Fernand blushed. "Finally."

"Marvellous!" Lucinda cried. "When is the happy event to be?"

"Another three months yet. But I did not want Dominique to travel."

"Ah," said Arthur. "You left Dominique behind so that your baby will be born in France, not England."

"*I* was born in France!" Fernand reminded them.

"Yes. In Les Carmes!"

"That is hardly my fault. Or my dear mother's. In the Revolution, in the Terror, everybody was thrown into prison. The best people were in Les Carmes!"

Lucinda pursed her lips. "What did Dominique say when you told her you were coming here without her?"

"I, er—" Fernand's hands moved expressively.

"You didn't tell her, did you?" deduced Arthur. "You sly old dog. You snuck across the Channel without telling Dominique. There is going to be hell to pay."

"Bah! There will not. Dominique was visiting her mother when I received Zoë's letter. She is not expected home for some time. The chances are she will not even know I have come. But just in case my stay was longer than anticipated, I left a note explaining..." His voice trailed away.

"Oh, Fernand, it is too good of you." She threw her arms around him again and kissed him once more. "That you should come tearing all the way from Château Niverne to Dorset! That you should leave Dominique's side—"

"—and for a pair of miscreants like us," Arthur completed. "Such a noble sacrifice!"

Fernand laughed. "You two are impossible!"

"Ah, that reminds me," Lucinda murmured. "I wonder if lunch will stretch to three."

"It reminds *me*," commented Arthur, "that we now have an excuse to get out of that wretched masquerade of Gabriel's."

Lucinda's heart sank.

"What masquerade is this?" enquired Fernand when Arthur had left the drawing room.

"We have had a casual invitation to the annual Midsummer Night's Ball at Sarne Abbey," explained Lucinda.

Fernand frowned. Such an invitation could only be issued by the owner of Sarne Abbey. "But the old Earl of Sarne is dead."

"The new one is very much alive, and was here to dinner last week."

"And he invited you both to this ball?"

"Yes. Melissa expressed a wish to see Sarne Abbey, and he mentioned the ball and invited everyone present. It was on the spur of the moment." She paused. "I don't suppose we shall be missed."

Even as she spoke, Lord Sarne's voice seemed to reverberate around her: *Promise me you'll come, Lucinda.* Her heart was thumping loudly. She hoped Fernand would not hear it.

But Fernand was watching her closely. He saw the faint blush steal up her alabaster cheeks. "And you wanted to go?"

Lucinda smiled coyly. "I'd rather spend the time with you, Fernand."

"I am honoured. However, you have not answered my question. If I were not here, would you want to go?"

Lucinda pouted. "I don't know. I would...and I wouldn't." She opened her brown eyes wide and gazed disarmingly at him. "Now, tell me, how is Dominique?"

The ensuing conversation never flagged. They talked unceasingly throughout lunch. The meal became less and less formal with each dish they tasted.

Fernand discarded his green jacket. Arthur shed his brown one. Their waistcoats were open, their cravats undone.

With Lucinda in a cotton dress, they raced outside to revisit their childhood haunts. They paddled in the stream and looked for minnows.

Lucinda shrieked as a frog leapt out of the long grass.

"Quick! Catch it!" cried Fernand. "We can have it for dinner!"

"Don't you dare!" shouted Arthur.

"What! You will not serve your brother a frog for dinner? What kind of hospitality is this?"

Arthur's answer was to knock his stepbrother off balance. They rolled in the grass under the old oak tree, playfully cuffing each other until they came too close to an ant heap and had to stick their feet in the stream to wash the insects away.

Lucinda, perched precariously on a mossy rock, laughed uproariously. Her straw hat was askew and her cinnamon curls tumbled onto her shoulders.

"And now, my dear Arthur," demanded Fernand, when they were drying off in the sun, "When are you going to marry?"

"Marry? Me?" countered Arthur. "I'm a bankrupt. A debtor. An impecunious wretch like me cannot get married. Think of England! The economy would die on its feet if I got married!"

Fernand chuckled. "What about you, Lucinda?"

A vision of the Earl of Sarne's dark, brooding face rose in her mind. He was out of her reach, she told herself firmly. A foreign princess will marry him—or an English heiress. In answer, she shook her head.

"What? No proposals? Nothing?" persisted Fernand.

"Not unless you count Sir Kirby Hookmeadow's." Lucinda joined them on the grassy knoll, placing herself between them.

"I heard someone say that he is not welcome here," Fernand remarked.

Arthur nodded. "The swine should be horsewhipped!"

Fernand raised an enquiring brow.

"He tried to take advantage of Lucinda," Arthur explained.

"Ah, very nasty," Fernand continued, "but this Lord Sarne—*Gabriel* you called him, as if you were friends—"

"A slip," said Arthur quickly. "He asked us to use his Christian name at dinner, since he and Lord Overberry were the only strangers and the rest of us were well acquainted."

"And having done it once," explained Lucinda, "we cannot go back."

"I doubt we shall see much of him in the future," Arthur added. "Once the auction is over, we shall not move in the same circles."

Fernand frowned. "You seem very casual about this auction."

"Casual? Us?"

"Zoë wrote that the auction was today."

"So it was," confirmed Lucinda. "At least, it was supposed to be."

Arthur pursed his lips. "We had some trouble with the printer. He made the date the twenty-eighth—next Monday."

Fernand sucked in his breath. "You cannot alter it?"

"Not now. It is too late," answered Lucinda. "Besides, it is only one week more. So it is not a disaster for us."

"*Mais, au contraire*! It is a blessing in disguise!" declared Fernand. "For you now have my company for an entire eight days!"

Lucinda flicked some water in his face. He veered away from her, laughing.

"Drat!" exclaimed Arthur. "My watch has stopped! Do you have the time, Fernand?"

Fernand glanced at the sun. "About four, I should think."

"Four—teatime." Arthur licked his lips. "The hour of seed cake, gooseberries and cream, cucumber sandwiches, currant bread and quince jelly."

"I'll race you back to the house!" Lucinda was already running up the hill.

Fernand caught her by the ankle. She gave a squeal as she sank onto the grass. Then she leaned forward and pushed Fernand. He lost his balance and fell backward, knocking Arthur over. Scrabbling wildly at blades of grass, the two men rolled almost into the stream below. Lucinda laughingly watched as they began to pick themselves up. Then she turned and continued to run up the hill as fast as she could go.

It was not until until she reached the top that she saw him.

He was mounted on a sorrel mare. His black boots were thrust into gleaming bronze stirrups. His legs, in grey breeches, tightly gripped the mahogany leather saddle. His scarlet coat was offset by the white ruffles of his shirt.

He swept off his grey beaver and bowed. "Good morning, Lucinda." Then his jet-black eyes roved over her.

Lucinda was suddenly aware of how disheveled she must look. Her hat hung behind her, her light brown curls loose and unkempt. Her dress was splashed with water and stained with mud, and she wore no shoes.

She curtseyed numbly. "Good afternoon, Gabriel."

CHAPTER SEVEN

THE EARL OF SARNE stared at her.

Lucinda coloured and hid her face. She did not know how adorable she looked. Her cheeks were flushed from healthy exercise. Her curls tempted him to run his fingers through them. Her dress—too large and slightly old-fashioned—was more enticing than the seven veils of Salome.

"Wh-what brings you here?" enquired Lucinda haltingly.

Lord Sarne's expression was suddenly bleak. "I received a note from your brother this morning, Lucinda," he answered. "He tells me that you are not coming to the Midsummer Night's Ball."

Lucinda nervously took her lip between her teeth. How quickly Arthur had acted. "We . . . we have a guest." Involuntarily she turned toward the hill.

Lord Sarne's sharp eyes followed her movement. "So the letter said."

Fernand staggered up, short of breath, but well ahead of Arthur. His linen shirt was undone, he carried his dripping wet stockings in his hand, and like Lucinda, he wore no shoes.

Lord Sarne's mouth tightened. He guessed the visitor was no ordinary one. He understood that this man had privileges denied to others, and so watched him like a hawk.

Fernand came to Lucinda's side. He smiled genially and bowed to the earl.

"May I present," Lucinda said awkwardly, "the Earl of Sarne? Le Marquis de Niverne, Lord Sarne."

Lord Sarne returned the bow. "Your servant."

"Yours, I am sure." Fernand bowed again. It was a florid bow, almost mocking in its execution. Casually, he draped his arm around Lucinda's shoulders.

Lord Sarne's black eyes flashed with anger at the gesture, and his voice was almost menacing as he said to Lucinda, "Any guest of yours is of course invited to my Midsummer Night's Ball. Please inform your brother that we look forward to seeing all of you at Sarne Abbey." He extended his hand. "I have some extra invitations. I hope you—and your brother—will make use of them."

Lucinda took them gingerly. "Th-thank you," she stammered.

Lord Sarne addressed Fernand. He smiled, but his smile seemed cold, haughty and arrogant. Perhaps even hostile. "I hope we shall have the pleasure of your company on Thursday...with the Edringtons."

Fernand offered a slight, formal bow in reply.

"The Midsummer Night's Ball at Sarne Abbey is not to be missed," added the earl. Then he wheeled his horse and galloped off.

Fernand swore softly.

"Fernand!" scolded Lucinda.

Fernand took his arm from her shoulder and shrugged.

"Wasn't that Gabriel riding off?" asked Arthur as he reached the brow of the hill.

"Yes," Lucinda answered flatly.

"What happened?" His eyes went from Lucinda to Fernand for an explanation.

"He has renewed his invitation for you and Lucinda to come to his Midsummer Night's Ball. He has also invited me."

"Damn!" burst out Arthur.

"Arthur!" Lucinda rebuked.

Arthur shrugged. "I'm sorry." Then he made a face. "Anything else?"

"Yes. He brought some extra invitations for us to use." Lucinda gave them to him.

Arthur heaved a deep sigh. "Oh, well, if Gabriel is *determined* we shall come, I suppose we had best go. There is no point in making an enemy of him."

"Exactly," agreed Fernand. "Besides, this Midsummer Night's Ball could be most . . . entertaining."

Arthur glanced sharply at him.

"Who knows?" Fernand's expression was bland. "You may find an heiress who will be prepared to marry you first thing on Friday morning."

Arthur started to laugh. "No such luck. Come. Let's go in and have some tea. My throat is as dry as parchment."

THE SUN WAS SETTING slowly. The ruins of the thirteenth-century Abbey of Sarne were bathed in a rich, golden glow. The diamond-paned windows of the rambling Tudor mansion which derived its name from

he Abbey, shone as if they contained thousands of
ose nobles.

The masqueraders arrived in daylight. Their cos-
umes covered every aspect of literature and mythol-
gy, of history and nature.

Lord Sarne received them. He was unmasked, and
a dinner dress. He'd lost count of the number of times
is guests had cried, "Oh, but you are not in cos-
ume!" Or, "Are you not going to dress up for the
ccasion?"

"I shall change after everyone has arrived," he in-
ariably replied. "That way no one will know who I
m."

The carriage carrying Lucinda, Fernand and Arthur
as but one of a long line of vehicles approaching the
ntrance to Sarne Abbey.

Lord Sarne's gaze penetrated his fair guest's mask.
Lucinda, is it not?"

"Tsk!" Lucinda clicked her tongue. "You have
ound me out. And I thought I had such an excellent
isguise."

Lord Sarne surveyed her.

There was a sparkling rose-quartz-and-diamond
ara upon her head. Her hair had been coiffed and
urled provocatively around it. A high-peaked,
equined mask hid her eyes. Her high-waisted deep-
ink gossamer silk gown was bordered by rows of ar-
ficial flowers and jewels. The sleeves were puffed at
he shoulders, then widened to a single fall of silk
hich ended at her wrists.

"It is exquisite," Lord Sarne allowed. "But who are
ou supposed to be?"

Lucinda pouted. "Titania. Titania from *A Midsummer Night's Dream*."

He laughed. "Of course. I should have guessed." He turned to Fernand and Arthur. "And which one of you two is Oberon?"

"Neither," replied Arthur. "I had thought to play Puck, but concluded that my idea of Puck's costume would get me thrown out."

Lord Sarne grinned and ignored the sniggers of those within hearing whose imaginations had run riot. "Who have you chosen to be instead?"

Arthur twisted a curl of his long, flowing wig. "Charles the First, our martyred majesty."

"Is that wise? He lost his head."

"So have I. Witness the auction of Bluebell Manor."

A burst of laughter came from his audience.

"And you, My Lord?" The Earl of Sarne addressed Fernand.

"I am the Lord of Misrule," he replied. "Fortune's Fool." He bowed with a flourish, displaying his wide grey-green sleeves, scattered with lozenge-shaped pea-green, coffee- and grape-coloured patches. His breeches were brown, like unpolished wood covered with hoar-frost. He wore doeskin boots with black tassels. "I have come instead of Puck to make as much mischief as I possibly can."

Lord Sarne seemed to have forgotten his former hostility toward Fernand and appeared richly amused. "You are welcome to stir up as much trouble among my guests as you like. And you will have plenty of

ime, for the unmasking will not be until seven tomorrow morning.''

Fernand smiled and bowed once more. Then the
three of them threaded their way among their fellow-
masqueraders, past liveried footmen and pert maids
and into the ballroom.

The orchestra was playing a lively waltz, and it was
not long before the company was dancing merrily.

AS THE EVENING WORE ON and the light outside faded,
the chandeliers were lit. The ballroom became sti-
flingly hot, and so the windows were opened. Then the
ball supper was announced.

Lucinda had been dancing with Fernand. ''I don't
really want to eat just yet,'' she said. ''But I am dying
for something to drink.''

''Yes, I am, too,'' replied Fernand. ''Let's go in and
see what they have.''

They were among the first to arrive in the supper
rooms upstairs. The tables groaned under the weight
of steaming hot white soup; beef sausages; slices of
cheese; veal-and-ham pie; hard-boiled eggs in curry
sauce; currant fritters; potted salmon; pyramids of
cherries; Chantilly cakes; ratafias; gingerbread; vanilla
ice; coffee cream; lemon sherbet; champagne; raisin
wine, claret, milk punch and orgeat.

''You would think,'' observed Fernand, ''that we
are expected to eat for the next nine days, instead of
merely the next nine hours!''

''It is less than you imagine. Believe me, it will dis-
appear in the twinkling of an eye,'' Lucinda assured
him.

Fernand considered. "You are perhaps right. I've never seen so many rotund men and tightly laced ladies! It must take mountains of food to support them."

"Don't be nasty, Fernand. *I* fully intend to have my fill. I won't let you shame me into starving myself upon ship's biscuits and soda water!"

"Good gracious! Lucinda!"

Lucinda turned to see who had addressed her. Facing her was a woman with a mass of false blond curls gleaming with jewels. Her gown was cloth of gold, its border so pinked, looped and ruffled that it defied description. It was her voice that gave her away. No one spoke quite like Bellemaine Anstruther.

"Belle!" declared Lucinda. "What a dazzling costume! Who are you meant to be?"

"Queen Guinevere," answered Bellemaine. "And you?"

"Titania."

"Ah! I thought I heard Gabriel say you were not coming—that you had a guest."

"Gabriel very kindly invited our guest, as well." Lucinda turned toward Fernand. "Miss Anstruther, may I present the Marquis de Niverne."

Bellemaine curtseyed.

Fernand bowed, took her hand and kissed her fingertips. *"Enchanté."*

Bellemaine smiled winsomely. "The Marquis de Niverne! You are French?"

"Every inch of me, *mademoiselle*."

"Pray do not be so formal." Bellemaine's eyelashes fluttered. "You must call me Belle. Everyone does. Then we can be friends."

"A thousand thanks. My name is Fernand." He kissed her hand once more.

"Fernand!" breathed Bellemaine. The word was like a caress. "Have you known Lucinda long?"

"All our lives."

"How strange. In all the years I have known Lucinda, she has never mentioned your name."

"Hasn't she?" Fernand was flirting as he always did. "How very remiss of her. Lucinda! How can you have neglected to mention me to your charming friend?"

"Yes, Lucinda. It is really too bad of you," admonished Belle.

"I did not think you would be interested, Belle," began Lucinda. "Fernand is—"

"How can you say such a thing, Lucinda!" interrupted Bellemaine. Laughingly she linked her arm with Fernand's. "Is she not wicked?"

"Never mind. We shall make up for it now."

"Yes, indeed. Come! Let me show you the delights of an English banquet."

Lucinda stared in amazement while Bellemaine whisked Fernand away.

"You are reluctant to let him go?"

The voice which sounded in Lucinda's ear belonged to the Earl of Sarne. She would have known it anywhere.

Abruptly, she faced him. He was now attired like a Barbary corsair. His dark hair was concealed by a scarlet bandanna, a gold earring dangled from one ear and his purple shirt was open to reveal his chest. Around his neck hung heavily jewelled gold and silver chains, like the plunder from a galley. His breeches were striped in red and white. And like Fernand, he wore boots of the finest leather.

But it was not the vivid costume which held her attention. She was riveted by his smouldering eyes.

"I..." Her tongue tripped over itself. "She— Belle—didn't let me finish. I—I wanted to say that Fernand is my brother."

Lord Sarne's eyebrow lifted. "Your brother?"

"Yes. My half brother."

Lord Sarne's gaze was as forbidding as a black cloud in a hurricane. At once he seized her arm. "Come!" he ordered.

Through the tide of excitement rising in her, Lucinda felt a twinge of fear. She did not dare to question him. As if in a trance, she let him lead her past the tables which were brimming with tempting morsels, pausing only once to take a glass of champagne.

They left the noisy throng and emerged onto a balcony which was cool and fragrant from the scented flowers winding around the stone balustrade.

"Wh-why did you bring me here?" Lucinda asked nervously.

Placing her at one end of a smooth marble bench, he flung himself down at its opposite end, his hands spread carelessly over the low stone wall behind.

"I am confused. I beseech you to enlighten me."

Lucinda sipped her champagne. "What, pray, has confused you?"

"You told me Arthur is your brother, or rather your half brother."

"He is."

"Yet the Marquis de Niverne is the same age as Arthur. How can he possibly be your half brother, as well?"

"Fernand is my mother's son. Arthur is my father's son."

Lord Sarne frowned. "How is that possible?"

Lucinda shrugged, then sipped more champagne. "'Tis a long story. I'm afraid it will bore you." Her glass was empty. She put it down and started to rise.

Lord Sarne caught her hand. His black eyes pleaded with her.

She sank down onto the marble bench once more, seemingly unaware that the distance between them had closed. The folds of her silken gown now fell over his legs.

"You will drive me mad!" he murmured passionately.

A slow flush mounted her throat and burst into flame across her cheeks. Her body tensed to spring and run away.

Then a smile dispersed the intensity of his words. "If you don't tell me the whole story," he added lightly.

Lucinda's demeanour became at once coquettish. "Very well."

He kissed her fingertips, sending a tingling ecstasy the length of her arm.

"M-my mother," she began after some thought, "Clotilde Touissant, was betrothed to Fernand, Marquis de Niverne. . . ."

"Fernand's father?"

"Yes."

"When?"

"It was in ninety-one. The situation in France even then was bad. With the flight of the King and Queen to Varennes, it became very much worse."

"I recall." His forehead wrinkled. "Wasn't there a Général de Niverne?"

"Yes. The Marquis de Niverne was a general in the French Army."

"He stayed?"

"He thought it would be better if he remained in France. He felt he might be able to use his position to help the Royal Family to escape. He had several plans, but neither the King nor the Queen would listen to him."

"Why not?"

"Who knows? They closed their ears to a number of people who were trying to help them. In any case, after the King's execution, the Marquis de Niverne supported a scheme to free Marie Antoinette. The plan failed. He and my mother went into hiding. After the fall of Danton, in April 1794, they were captured and imprisoned. In July, the marquis was executed. My mother was with child. . . ."

"So she escaped the guillotine?"

"Yes. Then Robespierre fell, and I think it was in September that my mother was released from Les Carmes. By that time she had given birth to Fernand, named after his father. His baptismal certificate—it was a piece of paper torn from a book—was witnessed by half the aristocracy in France!"

"It must be a fascinating document."

"Indeed it is," agreed Lucinda.

Lord Sarne's lips were parted in a smile. Lucinda was tempted to touch him, to allow her fingers to wander over his mouth...

It was with difficulty that she continued, "My mother decided that although Robespierre had fallen it was still not safe for her or for Fernand in France."

"So she came to England?"

"Exactly. Meanwhile, my father, Edgar Edrington, had married Hester Warton. That same year—1794—she gave birth to Arthur. She died in childbirth."

"I'm sorry."

"Thank you. Papa was very worried about Arthur. He wanted to find a wet-nurse for him, but he could not. And he was afraid Arthur would not live."

Lord Sarne's eyes darkened.

"By good fortune, he met my mother. They liked each other. Thus, after due consideration, they decided to marry and she nursed Arthur along with Fernand."

"As if they were twins."

"Yes. They grew up very close. Much closer than stepbrothers normally do."

"And you?"

"I was born three years later. And there you have it." She made as if to go.

Lord Sarne jumped to his feet. "Please," his voice was soft and beguiling, "go on."

CHAPTER EIGHT

LUCINDA SPREAD HER FAN and waved it before her heated face. "I shall bore you."

"Impossible," replied Lord Sarne.

"But my life story is so prosaic. So dull."

"It fascinates *me*."

She veiled her eyes with lashes. "*You* must have a more interesting story to tell."

"No. I have told you all there is. I can sum up my life in a few sentences." A strong arm curved round her. She could feel its heat through the sheer silk of her dress.

When she spoke again, her voice sounded a little breathless. "I am sure there must be more to your life...than that."

"Very little. If tales of battles amuse you, I could tell you a thousand. All filled with smoke and fire and the cries of the wounded. All preceded by long tedious waits in the hot sun, with flies settling on our noses and our sweat drying to salt on our bodies."

Lucinda offered a wry grimace.

"Or would you prefer to hear about the petty incidents which made my parents' marriage a living hell?" he asked bitterly.

"You must have had some happy times. With people like Vincent, perhaps?"

"Yes, indeed. I—" He studied her shrewdly. "So that is it! You wish to know about my *female* friends!"

Lucinda looked down at her dainty feet. It seemed the safest thing to do.

His arm fell away from her. He placed the toe of his boot upon the marble bench and leaned upon his right knee. "I don't deny I have had my fling."

Lucinda tapped her foot impatiently. "I did not expect you had grown up in a cloister."

"But you would have preferred it."

"Only if you would prefer me to have grown up in a convent."

"I had much, much rather *all* women grew up in convents."

Her brown eyes flashed furiously. "Of all the arrogant . . . !"

Then she saw his lips twitch and his black eyes sparkle with amusement, and her expression changed to a charming pout.

"I have a reputation—" He left the phrase unfinished, almost as if daring Lucinda to complete it. When she said nothing, he went on, "It has been greatly exaggerated."

"But there have been several—" Lucinda spread her slender hands wide "—ladies?"

The Earl of Sarne sighed. The light had gone out of his eyes. His mouth was set in a hard, tight line. "Do you really wish to hear about every treachery, every deceitful intrigue your sex can practise? Do you long to know of the jealousies and the betrayals? Do you care to learn of societies where honour means paying one's debts at cards, and fidelity means having only one lover?''

Lucinda was silent.

''Come sit down again,'' he coaxed, ''and fascinate me with the story of your childhood.''

Skilfully, he drew her once more onto the marble bench beside him. Her hands nestled in his. She was closer to him than ever before, and the warmth of his body seemed to envelope her.

''What do you wish to know?'' she whispered.

''Everything.''

''Oh, no, Gabriel! We should be here until we are both old and grey.''

He did not reply, but his look, as he raised her hands to his lips, spoke volumes.

Lucinda's heart did somersaults. Her mind was in turmoil. She had never known a man who could twist and turn her this way, she thought. He made her feel as if she were walking through a dream. . . .

Then he spoke. ''Did you ever go to France. . . as a child?''

''Yes.'' Her throat felt suddenly constricted, and the words came with difficulty. ''As soon as the Peace of Amiens was announced, we went at once to Niverne. Papa was determined that Fernand should not be deprived of his inheritance. He took us to see the Château Niverne. Mama made an official declaration that Fernand was the son of the late Marquis de Niverne.''

''Was there any doubt?''

Lucinda's brow furrowed. "I...I am not sure. It was probably a formality. But my parents both felt that Fernand's claim should be registered. They left a copy of the baptismal certificate with the authorities."

"Not the original?"

"No. They did not trust them."

Lord Sarne laughed. "Very wise. Especially with Bonaparte as First Consul!" He paused. "And I suppose the Consulate restored the Château to your half brother."

"Goodness, no! The authorities were surprised, and not at all pleased to learn about Fernand's existence. They had given the Château to a Monsieur Montreuille, a Bonapartist."

"So a long legal battle was started, I presume."

"Er, no. One probably would have been if the Peace of Amiens had lasted longer. But suddenly war was declared. An order was put out to arrest all Englishmen. Monsieur Montreuille was given the honour of arresting Papa."

Lord Sarne's eyes widened.

"We had to run for our lives," added Lucinda.

His hands tightened on hers. "Were you frightened?"

"Oh, no! It was very exciting! We found out about the order from a loyal servant of the late marquis. He still called Mama *Madame la Marquise*. He didn't know—nobody knew in France—that she was married to Papa. He brought the news to us just when we children were being put to bed at night. So of course we got to stay up late . . ."

"And that pleased you?"

"Very much. We had to help with the packing. The hustle and bustle was extraordinary. Everything was flung into our trunks. We could not get the lids down, and we had to sit on them while Papa tightened the straps. Then we had to creep out of our lodgings quietly with Mama and Papa saying 'sssh-sssh!' We thought it was very funny. We went around saying 'sssh-sssh!' to one another, too."

"You must have had a struggle not to giggle."

"Indeed we did."

"And then?"

"Mama and Papa led the horses out a little distance from the house. They harnessed them to a rickety carriage which must have been made in the days of Louis Quatorze. We were bundled in. Papa took the reins and we started north as fast as we could go."

"How long did the carriage last you?"

"Until daybreak. Then it fell to pieces. Wheels, hood and everything were scattered for miles."

"You exaggerate!"

"I do not!" She looked up in mock offence and was unaware of how nearly he came to crushing her to him. "Luckily we were near our destination—the seaport of Saint Brieuc. We found a boat which could take us from there to Cornwall. It had to be done at night. We hid under canvas, keeping quiet—" She halted. "It was great fun!"

"I would wager your parents didn't think so."

She laughed delightedly. "No, I'm sure they didn't. But we had no idea of the danger, only of the adventure."

She stopped speaking as she caught the expression in his eyes. His lips moved closer to hers. His arms tightened around her. Lucinda's hands slipped around his neck, drawing his head toward her. The kiss was delicious, like the freshness of a summer morning. It was too beautiful to stop. It should have gone on and on—

"Gabriel!" Nona Fitzjames's voice was strident, demanding. "Are you out there?"

Her hand rattled the balcony door.

Lucinda and Lord Sarne broke apart. Lucinda knocked the champagne glass from its perch. It smashed on the stones, scattering glass fragments in a wide arc.

A second later, Nona Fitzjames stood before them. "A messenger has arrived from London. From the Prince Regent."

Lord Sarne grimaced. "It will be government business." He sighed and said apologetically, "I shall have to deal with it immediately."

THE NIGHT WORE ON, and Lucinda danced until she was dizzy. It was an age before she returned to the supper rooms, and by then she was truly hungry. She disdained the white soup, and seized a slice of beef sausage. The currant fritters took her fancy. So did the gingerbread. She had a slice of cheese. A bite here, a nibble there.

The supper rooms were crowded now. Lucinda was jostled constantly by people shoving their way to the tables. And the noise of the other guests' talking, eating and drinking was almost deafening. She was glad to escape. She returned to the same balcony, for Lord Sarne had asked her to meet him there. "I shall look for you," he had promised, "at two o'clock."

Lucinda sat down on the marble bench. The shattered pieces of her champagne glass had been swept up. There was nothing to indicate that anyone had been there earlier that night.

Lucinda yawned. The wine was making her sleepy. Deciding to go for a cup of coffee, she opened the balcony doors.

"Ah! There you are at last!"

A strangled cry died in Lucinda's throat. It was not the earl but Sir Kirby Hookmeadow, in the costume of a Dominican monk. He looked evil and slightly depraved under the rough black hood.

CHAPTER NINE

SIR KIRBY CLOSED the doors behind them. "Lucinda, my dear. I have waited all evening for this opportunity to speak to you—alone."

"I have no wish to talk to you, Sir Kirby." Lucinda made as if to leave the balcony.

Sir Kirby blocked her way.

"Please, let me pass." She tried to slip round him. But he seized her wrist and twisted it so sharply that she gave a thin scream of pain.

"I made you a proposal of marriage," he growled. "Have you forgotten?"

"And I gave you my answer, Sir Kirby. It was no!"

"Ah, but you had not reflected properly upon it then."

"On the contrary, I had. My answer is still no."

"Poor child. You have not considered the consequences of your stubborn refusal, have you?" His smile was nauseating. "You will change your mind, Lucinda."

Lucinda shook her head, shivering with revulsion. She pushed at his fingers, trying to make him release her. But he was insensible to her silent plea.

"I can understand that your brother does not wish me to settle his debts. That is commendable. What is less, er, praiseworthy is that he has compelled you to, er, surrender your inheritance.''

"The choice was mine. Besides, we could not auction only half the estate.''

Sir Kirby smiled. ''You both fail to understand me. You need not auction Bluebell Manor at all.''

"What do you mean?''

"You could sell half of it—to your future husband.''

"Are you saying that you wish to buy Arthur's share and marry me?'' And thus, although she did not say it, acquire the whole of Bluebell Manor for half the price.

"Exactly. I am prepared to pay forty thousand pounds. A fine offer, is it not?''

Lucinda said nothing and Sir Kirby took her silence for consent. ''Let us seal the bargain with a kiss!''

"Don't touch me!'' Lucinda jerked back.

"Tut, tut. You are mine. I intend to have you.''

Behind them, the balcony doors were opened and Lord Sarne emerged. He saw Lucinda writhing in Sir Kirby's grasp. His fist connected with Sir Kirby's jaw, and the knight went sprawling. Then he grunted and staggered to his feet.

"I suggest,'' said Lord Sarne, with icy, suppressed fury, ''that you take the first opportunity to leave my house.''

Sir Kirby Hookmeadow's tiny, piglike eyes fastened on Lucinda. ''Are you coming with me, my dear?''

"Not if you were the last man alive!''

"You will regret those words!" snarled Sir Kirby. "I shall see to it!" And with that he stormed through the doorway into the house.

Lucinda collapsed onto the marble bench and started to weep. Tenderly, Lord Sarne put his arms around her. "Did he hurt you?" His voice was gentle, quite unlike the icy, cutting tone he had used toward Sir Kirby. "Lucinda, look at me!" He tilted her chin up and gazed deep into her tear-filled brown eyes. "Did he hurt you?"

She shook her head.

"It is as well he did not," murmured Lord Sarne, "for if he had, I would have killed him."

She gazed wonderingly at him.

His lips brushed hers. This time it was an almost brotherly kiss which felt comforting and soothing. "What did he say to upset you?"

"N-nothing."

"Tell me."

She drew a shuddering breath. "He wants Arthur and me to withdraw Bluebell Manor from the auction. He says he will buy Arthur out...for forty thousand pounds, if I will marry him." She almost choked on the words. "That way he would own half and his wife the other half."

Lord Sarne laughed. "The gall of the man! Where is he going to find the money?"

Lucinda stared. "I presume he has it...."

"Rubbish! His finances are shaky at best. He can't have that much capital available." He considered for a moment. "He must have applied to the bank for a loan. In that case, however, his credit will be stretched to the limit.'' He snorted contemptuously. ''Don't worry. He is not a threat to you.''

Lucinda heaved a sigh of relief. It was good to know that Sir Kirby Hookmeadow's schemes were doomed to failure. ''Thank you.'' Then she frowned.

''What is it?''

''This is the second time Sir Kirby has offered to buy Bluebell Manor. And both times he has tried to stop it going to other buyers. Why does he want it so much?''

Lord Sarne eyed her quizzically. ''It has certain...attractions.''

Lucinda acknowledged the compliment with a pretty smile. Then she asked, ''Did you settle that business of the Prince Regent's?''

''Easily,'' Lord Sarne responded carelessly.

Even as he spoke, the babble of voices inside increased. The rooms beyond the balcony were overflowing with his guests.

All at once two footmen flung open the balcony doors. Fresh air wafted in, to be greeted by a sigh of ecstasy from the revellers. From deep within the crowd, Bellemaine Anstruther caught sight of the Earl and Lucinda. Still with Fernand in tow, she came out to join them.

''I see you have found a cool place.''

''We have indeed. Come and join us,'' said Lord Sarne, rising.

''Thank you.'' Bellemaine sat down on the marble bench beside Lucinda. ''Were you having a pleasant tête-à-tête?''

Lord Sarne smiled. His black eyes met Lucinda's brown ones. A look of secret understanding passed between them.

He was about to speak, when Melissa lurched onto the balcony. Fernand put out his hand to steady her.

"Thank you." Melissa's speech was slurred. "I am obliged to you, sir."

Fernand kissed her hand. "I think you should sit down, *mademoiselle*."

"You are incorrect. I am *Madam*! Moreover, I am a queen!"

"Do sit down, Melissa!" pleaded Lucinda, immediately vacating her seat for her friend. "You look about to fall."

Even now Melissa was leaning dangerously far over the balustrade. Fernand was hanging on to her. But it would not have taken much to send her tumbling onto the terrace below.

Melissa faced her friend. "You need not worry, Lucinda," she assured her grandly. "I am perfectly all right."

"Allow me to escort you, Your Majesty!" Fernand guided Melissa to the marble bench.

She lowered herself with great care. Her steel-blue satin gown brushed against Bellemaine's golden ensemble. Her embroidered dancing slippers peeped out from under her frosted white petticoat.

Bellemaine surveyed her. "Who are you supposed to be, Melissa?"

"Marie Antoinette," answered Melissa. She struck her hand against her forehead. "A tragic queen!"

"But a very beautiful one," said Fernand.

"I know that voice—"

"You can't possibly," interjected Bellemaine. "This is the Marquis de Niverne. He—"

"Fernand!" gurgled Melissa delightedly. "What a strange costume you're wearing. I thought you would come as Bona . . . Bona . . . you know. Him."

"Bonaparte?"

"Yes."

"I came as the Lord of Misrule instead."

"You know each other?" enquired Lord Sarne with interest.

"Certainly!" exclaimed Melissa. "We always played together when we were children. Fernand and Arthur. Lucinda and me. *Hic!*"

"Really?" Bellemaine was skeptical. "I didn't know you had been to France as a child, Melissa."

"France? Why would I go to France? There was a war on. Couldn't go to France in the middle of a war. That's silly, Belle! I never went to France. I went to play with my friends. Dear, dear friends. Arthur, Fernand and Lucinda. Brothers and sister."

"Oh!" gasped Bellemaine in astonishment. She studied Fernand and Lucinda, noticing for the first time the family resemblance.

Melissa's eyes focussed blearily first on Bellemaine, then on Lucinda, and then on Fernand. "You are brothers and sister, aren't you?"

"Yes, of course," agreed Lucinda. "I—"

Bellemaine laughed suddenly. "I had no idea, Fernand, that you were Lucinda's brother!"

"Her half brother," corrected Fernand. "I would have told you, Belle, but your beauty made me forget everything else."

Bellemaine preened.

"Where is Dominique?" demanded Melissa.

"Dominique?" questioned Bellemaine.

"Fernand's wife."

"His . . . wife?"

Melissa nodded. "Fernand went to France. Got married. Dominique Something-or-other. Can't remember her name. It's this wig." She put her hands up to the white powdered wig which hid her own natural curls. "It muddles me."

"How unfortunate!" exclaimed Bellemaine softly.

There was a strange glint in her eyes, which Lucinda noticed, and for a moment it puzzled her. Then she dismissed it.

Bellemaine pointedly scrutinized her dance card.

Lord Sarne took the hint. "Belle, I believe you owe me a dance."

"Yes, I do, don't I, Gabriel?" Graciously she extended her hand to him. "Please excuse us."

As they reentered the salon, Lucinda gazed at Melissa.

"What you—what we—need, is some coffee."

"I shall fetch it," said Fernand.

He returned a few minutes later, announcing, *"Voilà le café!* And I have found Arthur."

"Oh, good," answered Lucinda. She took a cup. "Thank you, Fernand."

"Aren't you going to give Melissa any?" asked Arthur.

"Close the balcony doors, please, Arthur."

Arthur put the two cups he was carrying down on the parapet and did as Lucinda requested. "What is it?"

"She seems to have fainted."

Arthur surveyed Melissa. Her head was resting on her arm. Her eyes were closed. As her breast rose and fell, her diamond necklace sparkled brightly. "Oh, Lord!"

"What are we going to do?" asked Fernand.

"I shall take her home," decided Arthur.

"You?" countered Lucinda.

"Yes, why not? Someone must."

"She has servants . . . ." began Fernand.

"You can't leave her to servants! Not like this!" insisted Arthur. "Look at the jewels she is wearing—that diamond necklace, those sapphire bracelets." He shook his head vigorously. "I'll have her carriage sent for. Then I'll take her home."

When at last Arthur reappeared, having arranged for the carriage, he picked Melissa up in his arms with the ease of one who has spent his whole life doing that sort of thing.

Melissa was still dead to the world. One arm was draped gracefully over Arthur's shoulders. The other hung limply at her side. Her head rested on his chest, and she looked quite as if she belonged there.

"Why are you smiling, Lucinda?" demanded Arthur suspiciously.

"Melissa looks . . . awfully comfortable," Lucinda observed. "If I didn't know better, I would say she planned this."

Arthur gave a disgusted snort, spun on his heel and strode purposefully into the crowd.

THE UNMASKING took place in the early hours of a very rainy twenty-fifth of June.

There were gasps and squeals as people discovered whom they had been dancing with. Bursts of laughter echoed as folk realized what their friends and relatives had been wearing.

Then came the great departure. A procession of carriages began to wind its way across the countryside with every hood raised against the steady patter of raindrops.

In her own carriage with Fernand, Lucinda yawned as Bluebell Manor came in sight. "I *am* tired. Lucky Arthur—he has been in bed sleeping for at least two hours!"

"I don't think so," Fernand remarked. "Isn't that him riding toward us now?"

Lucinda pressed her face against the carriage window. A horseman in the costume of the early seventeenth century was galloping over the fields from Bush Hall. It could only be Arthur on the horse which he had borrowed from their carriage, leaving them one short.

"I believe you're right." Her forehead creased. "I wonder why it took him so long."

Fernand shrugged. "We'll soon find out."

Their carriage had already drawn up in front of the house. The footman opened the door and lowered the steps. Fernand jumped down and offered his arm to Lucinda.

As they entered the hall, Hebe met them. She
dropped a curtsey and gestured urgently in the direction of the drawing room.

Lucinda frowned, and opened the drawing-room
doors. There, sitting upright on the sofa in an ash-grey
negligée that could only have come from Paris, was
Dominique, Marquise de Niverne.

Her red curls shook with fury, and her green eyes
blazed with anger. She was not looking at Lucinda,
but past her at Fernand. "Where have you been?" she
demanded.

"Dominique!" Fernand looked as if the rug had
been whipped out from under him and he was struggling valiantly to save his balance.

"Don't 'Dominique' me!" his wife retorted. "You
steal off to England while I am visiting my mother.
There can be only one reason! Who is she?"

Fernand spread his arms wide. "But there is no one,
Dominique. I swear!"

"I don't believe you!" Dominique spat like a wild
cat. Confined by her pregnancy she might be, subdued by it she was not. "There is someone else. And I
want to know the name of the scheming whore!"

CHAPTER TEN

LUCINDA BACKED AWAY from the pitched battle. She locked the drawing-room doors behind her. Then, after a moment's thought, she slid the key underneath them.

A smile played about her lips. Monsieur Montreuille, to whom the Bonapartist regime had awarded the Château Niverne, had had a daughter, Dominique. When the Bourbons had been restored, it had seemed a good idea to Monsieur Montreuille to arrange a marriage between his daughter and the new marquis. Lucinda recalled how Dominique and Fernand had fought all the way to the altar. It was, of course, a love match.

In the middle of her reverie, the front door slammed violently.

Lucinda jumped. "Arthur, you frightened me. Good morning."

Arthur scowled. He dropped his hat, his wig and his long seventeenth-century cloak into Hebe's hands. "There is nothing *good* about it."

Lucinda opened her mouth to protest.

"Don't speak to me! I want a nice, hot bath and a long sleep." He sent the servants scurrying in every direction.

Lucinda followed him upstairs. "What happened?"

Arthur favoured her with a wry grimace. "Melissa woke up."

"That's wonderful."

"No, it is not wonderful!" he snapped. "She put her arms around my neck and kissed me. She told me I was the only man in the world for her. She said she loved me!"

Lucinda laughed. "You can't object to that, can you?"

"She wasn't herself," growled Arthur. "She didn't know what she was saying."

Lucinda blinked. "You mean, if Melissa had been herself, you would have liked it, but since she was—"

"Don't try to confuse me, Lucinda. I'm cross. Don't try to humour me. I am in no mood to be humoured."

"I wouldn't dream of humouring you. You can be as cross as you like."

Arthur grunted.

"But not in the drawing room."

Arthur stopped and stared at her. "Why not?"

"Because Dominique is in there tearing Fernand to shreds, and as their hosts, I feel we should wait until they are finished."

Arthur's scowl vanished. He started to laugh: "Give Dominique my love. I'll see her when I'm, er, human again!"

BLUEBELL MANOR was as quiet as the grave when Lucinda came downstairs that afternoon. Tenta tively, she tried the drawing room doors. They opened easily. She went in.

Dominique was still seated on the sofa. Her feet were now resting on a crimson-tapestried stool. Seeing Lucinda, she put her finger to her lips.

Beside her, curled up under a mountain of rugs, trusting as a child, was Fernand.

"Hush! Don't wake him!" Dominique exhorted her.

Lucinda smiled. So that quarrel was settled. Peace reigned—until the next time.

She bent down and exchanged kisses with her sister-in-law.

"Fernand had a hard night. He has been so very worried." Dominique took her lip between her teeth. "I couldn't understand it—something about how you must sell Bluebell Manor? An auction?"

Lucinda nodded. "Arthur placed some bets. He lost—"

"He lost? That is not like Arthur. There was a woman, no?" Dominique always suspected a woman.

Lucinda's delicate features clouded. "Bellemaine Anstruther. Arthur... Arthur wanted our fortune to match hers. He was going to propose, but instead—"

"Pffft!" Dominique concluded dramatically. "So, now you must sell?"

"Yes. The auction is on Monday. We don't know what kind of price we will get, nor who will buy Bluebell Manor..."

"And afterward? When this is settled? You will come to us? Yes?"

"If you will have us."

"Naturally, we will have you! Where else would you go? You are part of our family! Families must stick together!"

"ZOE!" cried Lucinda.

"Lucinda!" Zoë Joliffe enveloped her friend. "You'll never guess where I have been!"

"I shan't even try. Where?"

"To a royal christening at Kensington Palace, if you please! Aren't you just green with envy?"

Her cherry-red riding ensemble swished as she draped herself over a chair. Beside it, Lucinda's own pale grey striped muslin gown looked as dull as the clouds scudding across the sky that Saturday morning.

"Absolutely!" Brown eyes sparkling, she dropped into the chair opposite her friend. "You must tell me about it!"

"I intend to! But first I shall scold you for that miserable little letter you sent me, Lucinda! Only two lines and not a hint that the Earl of Sarne has returned! How could you keep such a juicy titbit from me?"

"It slipped my mind."

"Slipped your mind? Oooh-ooh-ooh!" wailed Zoë in exasperation. "Have you seen him? They say he is called the Black Earl because he is so dark. Is he?"

"One could say so. If the Bushens have invited you to their musical evening tonight..."

"They have."

"...then you will be able to see him and judge for yourself."

"Really?" Zoë's eyes gleamed in anticipation.

"I can't promise, mind. But his friend, Vincent—Lord Overberry—is staying with the Bushens and trying to marry Melissa."

"*Trying* to marry? Won't she have him?"

"No."

"Why not?"

"Because she does not choose to do so. But, as I was saying," Lucinda plowed on, firmly preventing Zoë from diverting her, "it is very likely that to please Vincent, Mr. and Mrs. Bushens will include Lord Sarne among their guests."

"Aha! Now tell me—what is the matter with Lord Overberry?"

"Nothing." Lucinda's lips twitched. "Except that he wears Cossacks."

"Why shouldn't he? They are the height of fashion!"

"Oh Zoë! Really!" Lucinda smothered a giggle. "They look so ridiculous!"

Zoë shrugged. "*You* may find them ridiculous. *I* find them elegant and charming."

"You are joking! You *cannot* like Cossacks!"

"I *do* like Cossacks. I much prefer them to those tightly moulded breeches which so many of the opposite sex wear. Why, every time a gentleman sits down wearing tight breeches, I worry myself to death in case the strain should prove too much!"

Lucinda burst into peals of laughter.

"There you are, you see!" Zoë was triumphant. "At least one knows that Cossacks will survive the operation of sitting down!" She waited until Lucinda had recovered before she went on. "So apart from his dress, where do you find fault with Lord Overberry?"

"There is no fault to be found with him. He is well mannered. He is as fair as Lord Sarne is dark. He has a promising career in the Horse Guards. And he is greatly respected."

"As fair as Lord Sarne is dark," murmured Zoë.

"What is it, Zoë?" Lucinda read her friend's expression. "Do you know him?"

"I may do. I met a man once—I did not know his name, for there wasn't a chance for an introduction. . . ." A dreamy look crossed her face. "Does Melissa really not wish to marry him?"

"Definitely not!"

"What about you?"

"No. We neither of us look on him in that way. We could love him as a brother. Or a friend. But not as a husband."

"Hmmm. If he is who I think he is . . ." Zoë paused and peeped at Lucinda from under her lashes.

"Melissa will be eternally grateful if you win Vincent for yourself," Lucinda assured her. "She has already refused him once, and she does not wish to hurt him with a second refusal. I shall be pleased, too, for I should like to see him happy. We should both be delighted to greet you as Lady Overberry."

"Thank you." Zoë smiled blissfully. "I'm glad there will not be any, er, unpleasantness."

Lucinda watched her for a moment while her thoughts drifted far away and dwelt upon pleasant recollections. Then she said: "Now, tell me about the christening."

"Christening?" Arthur had just come into the room. "What christening?"

Instead of answering, Zoë leapt to her feet. "Arthur, my love!" She threw herself into his arms and kissed him on both cheeks. "And Fernand! You came! I'm so pleased!" Fernand too was heartily embraced. "Dominique!" Zoë's grey eyes widened as she stared at Dominique's figure. "My goodness, you must have had difficulty travelling!"

Dominique shrugged. She kissed Zoë affectionately. "So you have come to mourn with us?"

"Mourn with you?" Zoë seemed surprised. She turned to Lucinda enquiringly. The light caught the gold braid trimming her military-style jacket.

"The auction is on Monday," clarified Lucinda.

"Yes! Isn't it exciting!"

"Exciting?" repeated Fernand, dazed.

"Definitely! To sell a house and not know who is going to have it, or what it will fetch! Wildly exciting! Great fun!"

Dominique had by now seated herself. The other ladies followed suit. The gentlemen were ranged around them.

"Now, tell us," requested Arthur, "whose christening did you attend?"

"One of the royal babies who cost you a fortune," answered Zoë.

"Which one?"

"Kent's. 'Tis the only one born in England. I thought you knew."

"Harrumph! The girl."

Zoë inclined her head in acknowledgement. "And you'll never believe the fuss there has been over her!"

"What fuss could there be at a christening?" asked Dominique, who occupied half the sofa. Fernand was beside her. His arm was around what would have been her waist, if she had not been with child.

"First, before the christening," Zoë began, "the Duke of Kent put the Prince Regent's back up by introducing his daughter to all and sundry as the next Queen of England."

"Oh, no!" gasped Lucinda.

"Oh, yes!" confirmed Zoë.

Arthur was making calculations. "But there are a dozen people between the princess and the throne! The Prince Regent," he enumerated, "the Duke of York, the Duke of Clarence..."

"And if the Clarences have any children," Lucinda chimed in, "she will drop even further down the line. Besides which, if the Kents have a son, she will be displaced."

"Does the Duke of Kent seriously believe what he said?" enquired Fernand.

Zoë shrugged. "As to that I cannot say. He may believe it, or he may simply have said it to annoy his brother. They don't get on."

"No. Kent's a pompous ass," commented Arthur. "While the Prince Regent is—"

"What's the child called?" Lucinda was determined to steer the conversation back on course.

"The Duke and Duchess of Kent wanted her christened Georgiana Charlotte Augusta Alexandrina Victoria."

"Poor girl!" said Arthur feelingly. He rose to his feet and pulled the bell-rope. "Would you like some refreshment? Sherry? A slice of cake?"

"Yes, please," answered Zoë. "I am hot and dusty from my ride. My baggage comes apace. I do hope I may stay with you! I must go to your auction. I wouldn't miss it for the world."

"Of course you may stay with us," Lucinda replied. "We have plenty of room and you know you are always welcome."

"Good. Because I told my carriages to come here."

"Carriages? Plural?" questioned Fernand.

Zoë looked down her nose at him. "You don't expect me to travel with only *one* carriage do you?"

Fernand gazed at her with fascinated horror.

"Zoë never travels lightly," quipped Arthur.

CHAPTER ELEVEN

IT WAS SATURDAY EVENING. The music room at Bush Hall was draped with peach velvet. The violins had been laid down. The pianoforte had been abandoned.

"They held the christening in the Cupola Room," Zoë was saying, "in the state apartments of Kensington Palace."

Zoë had declined to sing. "My voice is very loud and flat and cracks on the high notes. And I don't play."

"Tell us about the royal christening instead," Arthur had suggested.

"Yes, do!" Melissa had supported him.

From then on every eye was fixed on Zoë, especially Lord Overberry's. He was seated nearly opposite her and it was plain to see that since she had burst into their midst, he had eyes for no other woman.

"The Cupola Room is square," Zoë said, setting the scene, "with Greek columns painted a shade of—" she searched for a word. "—pale gold. The ceiling is covered with blue medallions painted on a white ground. It is at least two hundred feet high—"

"Impossible!" interrupted Lord Sarne. "I've seen the outside of Kensington Palace. There is no height to it."

Zoë sighed. "Oh, dear. Then it is an optical illusion. Pity. Still, it is very effective." She smiled brightly and continued, "There is a white marble fireplace on one side and white niches filled with gold statues of the gods and goddesses of antiquity. In the middle of the room is a golden font."

"Vulgar," decided Mr. Bushens.

Zoë ignored him. "The Archbishop of Canterbury held the baby in his arms. Such a tiny little thing she is—you wouldn't believe how small!"

"That's a bad sign!" declared Mrs. Bushens. "The child will not survive long if she is too small. Mark my words, she'll be dead within a year!"

"That's as may be. I don't know, I'm sure. As I said, they were going to call her Georgiana Charlotte Augusta Alexandrina Victoria, and the Archbishop was waiting for the Prince Regent, who was one of the godfathers, to name her. But His Royal Highness wouldn't say anything."

"What?" asked Arthur. "Not a word?"

"Not a word. Mind you, it was the Duke of Kent's fault. He wanted his daughter's other godfather to be the Tsar of Russia, which offended the Prince Regent greatly."

"Perhaps he didn't realize..." began Bellemaine.

"Oh, he knew perfectly well, for he is always telling people how he heard some poor unfortunate ask the Prince Regent what he thought of the Tsar. And the Prince Regent answered—"

"'I hate him! God damn him!'" completed Lord Overberry.

"Oh!" Mrs. Bushens's hands fluttered to her ears as if to prevent the words from assailing them.

"Really, sir!" scolded Mr. Bushens.

Lord Overberry went pink and muttered an apology.

Melissa fanned herself with a glittering black fan which set off her fashionably ruched black dress to perfection. "I suppose that means the Russian Ambassador and his wife were present—the ones with that ridiculous name—Leeven...Leeayvin. ...I never do know how to pronounce it."

"Neither do I," agreed Zoë, "though I call her 'Leaving' because I wish she would. Yes. She was there. I noticed her because I particularly detest her."

"Why?" Bellemaine wanted to know.

"Anyone who has an unpronounceable name like that deserves to be detested. Besides, it is rumoured—" Zoë lowered her voice to the merest whisper "—that she betrays both Britain and Russia to her Austrian lover, Prince Metternich."

The shocked silence was broken by Lord Overberry. "I have heard it said that the Princess Lieven is both witty and attractive."

"She is well spoken of by your sex," conceded Zoë, "but I can't understand what you see in her, I must confess. I pity her poor husband. To be the Tsar's Ambassador in London with such a wife!"

"Zoë! The christening!" Arthur reminded her.

Zoë smiled at him. "Finally," she proceeded, "the Prince Regent said 'Alexandrina.' Then he stopped. Then the Duke of Kent tactlessly—so very tactlessly—suggested Charlotte. You know of course, how heartbroken the Prince Regent was after Princess Charlotte's death. Besides, it was the name of the Queen, his mother, and she is not even cold in her grave!''

"You exaggerate, Zoë!" exclaimed Arthur.

"Pooh! It was offensive. The Duke of Kent must have known that the Prince Regent would object! Anyway, the Duke of Kent then wanted Augusta. And after what he has been saying about his baby daughter being the next Queen of England..."

"He ought to have seen that the name would have been refused,'' commented Dominique. Her silver-tissue shawl was drawn over a green dress that matched her eyes. Her pregnancy was hardly noticeable.

"Then the Duke of Kent suggested Georgiana,'' continued Zoë, "and the Prince Regent gave him such a look! 'May I remind you,' said he, 'that I have already told you once, my name cannot be used, as I do not choose to place it before the Emperor of Russia's and I cannot allow it to follow.'"

Bellemaine frowned. "I do not understand that. Why not?"

"To put his own name before the Tsar's,'' explained Lord Sarne, "would have been extremely discourteous, since the Tsar is an Emperor while the Prince Regent is not yet a reigning monarch.''

"And His Royal Highness is never discourteous,'' added Lord Overberry.

"Of course. Thank you, er, both,'' responded Bellemaine. "But why not after?"

"The Prince Regent found it difficult enough," answered Lord Sarne, "to have to name the child after the Tsar in the first place. He could not but recall how abominably Alexander behaved to him when he visited England in 1814. But the Tsar was the baby's other godfather, so the Prince Regent swallowed his pride. He even graciously placed the Tsar's name first . . ."

"Yes, I see that, but—"

Lord Sarne held up one hand, commanding silence. "Having done as the parents wished and called her Alexandrina, the Prince Regent could not give her his own name. The humiliation of having his own name—and incidentally that of his forefathers—trailing after the name of so ill-mannered a brute, would have been intolerable!"

"Oh, I see."

"Do go on, Zoë!" urged Melissa.

"By this time," continued Zoë, "the Duchess of Kent was in tears. She never wanted the quarrel between the duke and his brother, and she knew as well as the next person that it was entirely the duke's fault!"

"Quite!" declared Lord Overberry.

"The Prince Regent then said, 'Call her after her mother.' I, personally, thought it was a sensible suggestion, and very kind to the Duchess of Kent."

In the background someone called "Hear! Hear!"

"So the Archbishop of Canterbury named her Alexandrina-Victoria, and the christening was completed. That, alas, was not the end of it. When I left London, that wretched Princess Lieven had spread at least six versions of the story—all putting the Prince Regent in the worst possible light!''

"Monstrous!'' If Lord Overberry had leaned any further forward in his chair, he would have fallen at her feet.

"Despicable!'' cried Mr. Bushens.

"What is the Prince Regent going to do about it?'' enquired Mrs. Bushens.

Zoë shrugged.

The Earl of Sarne ran his hand worriedly through his black hair. "He will probably do his best to avoid the Duke of Kent, which means he will turn for companionship to his other brothers.''

"York, Clarence and Sussex, you mean?'' questioned Mr. Bushens.

"Yes, and Cumberland.''

"Oh, heaven forbid!'' exclaimed their hostess. "We must pray that the Duchess of Kent will use her influence to smooth things over, and that no one will pay heed to that dreadful Princess Lieven!''

"Amen!'' chorused the others.

"And now,'' continued Mrs. Bushens, smiling broadly, "perhaps we can have another song? I don't believe you have performed for us, Belle.''

Bellemaine Anstruther glowed, and selected a German song, the name of which Lucinda did not catch.

"I shall accompany you.'' Mr. Bushens went to the pianoforte.

There was a clattering of chairs as the seating arrangements were changed. Lord Overberry made a

beeline for Zoë. He was skilfully outmanoeuvred by
Mrs. Bushens.

"There is a place here, Vincent."

Lord Overberry bowed and acquiesced, seating
himself, as his hostess wished, beside Melissa. That he
did it with reluctance was only too evident.

As soon as the reshuffling of chairs was over, Bellemaine began to sing. She had a good voice: pleasing,
strong, melodic.

Lucinda applauded enthusiastically as Bellemaine
finished. "You must sing us something else!" Anything, she thought, to stop Arthur taking up the vio-
lin again!

"Yes. Yes. Please do!" seconded Arthur. Anything, he thought, to prevent Lucinda playing the only
other passable piece in her repertoire—a tune he had
heard at least fifty times too often already!

"Oh, but I don't wish to monopolize...." protested Bellemaine modestly.

"Not at all." Lord Sarne was on his feet. "Let us
sing a duet." He leafed quickly through a sheaf of
music. "Here, what about this?"

Lucinda lamented that German had never been her
best language. Not only did she miss the name of the
tune, she also missed the significance of its soft, sweet
words.

Again there was rapturous applause.

"Delightful!" declared Mrs. Bushens. "Your voices
are perfectly blended." She turned to Lord Overberry. "Will you play or sing for us?"

Lord Overberry hesitated.

"Perhaps you could accompany Melissa?"

NOW THAT THE DOOR IS OPEN...
Peel off the bouquet and send it on the postpaid order card to receive:

4 FREE BOOKS
from

Harlequin Regency Romance ™

An attractive 20k gold electroplated chain FREE! And a mystery gift as an EXTRA BONUS!

PLUS

FREE HOME DELIVERY!

Once you receive your 4 FREE books and gifts, you'll be able to open your door to more great romance reading month after month. Enjoy the convenience of previewing 4 brand-new books every other month delivered right to your home months before they appear in stores. Each book is yours for the low member's only price of $2.49* — that's 26 cents off the retail cover price — with no additional charges for home delivery.

SPECIAL EXTRAS — FREE!

You'll also receive the "Heart to Heart" Newsletter FREE with every book shipment. Every issue is filled with interviews, news about upcoming books and more! And as a valued reader, we'll be sending you additional free gifts from time to time — as a token of our appreciation.

NO-RISK GUARANTEE!

- There's no obligation to buy — and the free books and gifts are yours to keep forever.
- You pay the low members' only price and receive books months before they appear in stores.
- You may cancel at any time, for any reason, just by sending us a note or shipping statement marked "cancel" or by returning any shipment of books to us at our cost. Either way the free books and gifts are yours to keep!

RETURN THE POSTPAID ORDER CARD TODAY AND OPEN YOUR DOOR TO THESE 4 EXCITING LOVE-FILLED NOVELS. THEY ARE YOURS ABSOLUTELY FREE ALONG WITH YOUR 20k GOLD ELECTROPLATED CHAIN AND MYSTERY GIFT.

*Terms and prices subject to change without notice.
Sales tax applicable in NY and Iowa.
© 1989 Harlequin Enterprises Ltd.

HARLEQUIN READER SERVICE
901 FUHRMANN BLVD
PO BOX 1867
BUFFALO NY 14240-9952

Place the Bouquet here →

Yes! I have attached the bouquet above. Please rush me my four Harlequin REGENCY™ novels along with my FREE 20k Electroplated Gold Chain and mystery gift as explained on the opposite page. I understand that accepting these books and gifts places me under no obligation ever to buy any books. I may cancel at any time for any reason, and the free books and gifts will be mine to keep!   248 CIH 4AJH (U-H-RG-02/90)

Name _____

Address _____ Apt. _____

City _____ State _____

Zip _____

Offer limited to one per household and not valid for present Harlequin Regency subscribers. Terms and prices subject to change without notice. Orders subject to approval.

© 1989 Harlequin Enterprises Ltd.   PRINTED IN U.S.A.

Take this beautiful
20k GOLD
ELECTROPLATED CHAIN
with your 4 FREE BOOKS
PLUS A MYSTERY GIFT

BUSINESS REPLY CARD

First Class   Permit No. 717   Buffalo, NY

Postage will be paid by addressee

**HARLEQUIN READER SERVICE
901 FUHRMANN BLVD
PO BOX 1867
BUFFALO NY 14240-9952**

NO POSTAGE
NECESSARY
IF MAILED
IN THE
UNITED STATES

Lord Overberry complied.

Melissa smiled winningly at her audience. Her voice was high, but it was not strong. Lucinda was glad for her sake she had chosen a short song. When she finished there was polite applause.

Melissa addressed her parents. "I think we might have some refreshment now, don't you?" As they murmured their agreement, she started toward the door, collecting Arthur en route.

Mr. and Mrs. Bushens glared at their daughter. Tight-lipped, they watched while Lord Overberry escorted Zoë, Lord Sarne offered his arm to Bellemaine and Fernand took Dominique and Lucinda.

Mr. and Mrs. Bushens spent the rest of the evening trying desperately to prise Lord Overberry loose from Zoë and throw him back into Melissa's arms. It was not to be.

At one point, Mrs. Bushens, her face as black as thunder, hauled Melissa to one side. "How can you!" Lucinda heard her say. "Don't you see Vincent is slipping away from you?"

Melissa glanced at her mother. "But, Mama, I told you. I don't love Vincent. I can't marry him."

"Rubbish. Marriage has nothing to do with love. Vincent will suit you very well."

"That's just it, Mama. He won't."

"He'll propose to Zoë Joliffe if you aren't careful!"

"Yes, Mama. And believe me I shall be very happy for both of them if he does."

Mrs. Bushens spluttered with rage. "Ungrateful child! Is this the thanks your father and I receive for trying to find you a worthy husband? Go to him at once!"

Melissa shrugged. Languidly she approached Lord Overberry. "Zoë tells me that you knew each other before you met here tonight."

Lord Overberry smiled at her. "Yes. That is true. Well...we didn't *know* each other—" his gaze strayed to Zoë "—we met, but there was no chance of a proper introduction."

"How very mysterious you make it sound!"

"It wasn't mysterious at all," countered Zoë. "It happened during Lady Tayce Vernon's fête—the one she gave before she went to America. Vincent and I— well, to tell the truth, someone jostled my arm and I spilled champagne over him!"

Melissa laughed delightedly. "Were you very angry with her?"

Lord Overberry shook his head. "She bewitched me from the start. I tried to seek a proper introduction, but her friends whipped her away."

"They saw my acute embarrassment!" interposed Zoë.

"And I spent the next three years searching for her," Lord Overberry went on. "I gave up hope...."

"So you came to Dorset to stay with us," Melissa suggested helpfully.

Lord Overberry nodded. "You can imagine how I felt when Zoë appeared here tonight!"

"How romantic!" exclaimed Melissa. "And you felt the same way?"

"Yes!" Zoë breathed ecstatically.

Melissa smiled benignly at them. "Look!" she cried. "How beautiful the moon is tonight. We have a nightingale that sings exquisitely when the moon is out. You must come and hear it, my dears."

Mrs. Bushens gave a horrified squawk as the three of them left the room. She prepared to charge after them, but Lord Sarne stood in front of her.

"Mrs. Bushens, I believe that there is an excellent portrait of you painted by the celebrated Zoffany at the time of your marriage."

"Yes. There is." Mrs. Bushens glanced anxiously, first round one of his broad shoulders, and then round the other.

Melissa, Zoë and Lord Overberry were almost out of sight, and Melissa's expression was enough to warn her that Zoë and Lord Overberry would not be chaperoned for long.

"I have heard that you were one of the most beautiful women in England," remarked the earl. "I must say it is easy to see why."

Mrs. Bushens blushed. "You flatter me."

"Not at all."

"How kind of you to say so."

"I wonder... may one see that picture?"

"Well, I... That is..." Mrs. Bushens was shaking with agitation. "It is upstairs, and..."

"It is no matter." Bellemaine had slipped her arm through Lord Sarne's. "We would love to see it."

Mrs. Bushens's face fell. "Oh." She recovered herself quickly. "I do hope you won't be disappointed," she added as she led them away from the others.

"I am sure we won't be," Lord Sarne replied.

Mr. Bushens, engaged in an earnest discussion with Arthur about the merits of Handel versus Mozart, suddenly realized that both Zoë and Lord Overberry were absent.

Recalling the strict instructions he had had from his wife not to allow such a thing to occur, he leapt to his feet and prepared to shepherd them back into the fold.

Then he saw that his wife had also disappeared. And his daughter was no longer in the room. He chewed his lip. He could not leave. Etiquette demanded that he remain with his guests.

Lord Sarne, Bellemaine and Mrs. Bushens returned some fifteen minutes later. Melissa came in after them, smiling like a cat that had been at the cream.

"Where is Vincent?" asked Mrs. Bushens with false brightness. "You are not neglecting him, are you, Melissa?"

"Oh, no, Mama," replied Melissa. "He is still on the terrace, enjoying the, er, moonlight."

"What, out there alone? For shame. Go and bring him in!"

"I wouldn't advise that, Mrs. Bushens," commented Lord Sarne.

"Oh? Why not?" demanded Mr. Bushens aggressively.

"Because he is talking to Zoë," answered the earl. "I could see them from the upstairs window, and their conversation is, er, of a private nature."

"Private? Nonsense! I'll fetch them myself."

Lord Sarne rested his fingertips gently, but restrainingly, on his host's sleeve. "Vincent has waited a long time for this moment. He saw Zoë once at a fête, but he lost her. Now that he has found her again he should be allowed to propose to her without interruption."

Mr. Bushens turned the same colour of red as his bristling moustache. "Propose to Zoë! But he came here to propose to Melissa!"

"And I refused him, Papa," Melissa reminded him.

"I don't know why you did not accept Vincent!" declared Mrs. Bushens. "He is a fine man."

"Excellent," conceded Melissa. "He'll make Zoë a wonderful husband. Don't you agree, Gabriel?"

"Absolutely," answered Lord Sarne.

Seconds later, Lord Overberry and Zoë reappeared through the French doors. It was evident from her blush that he had proposed. It was evident from his that she had accepted.

Melissa's parents fumed impotently as they realized that yet another peer had slipped from their daughter's grasp. Was there no way she could acquire a titled husband?

Even as the thought crossed their minds, Lord Overberry started to speak. "I have great pleasure in informing you," he announced unnecessarily, "that Miss Zoë Joliffe has consented to become my wife."

"How wonderful!" Melissa flung her arms around Zoë. "I'm so happy for you!" She kissed Lord Overberry on both cheeks. "Isn't this marvellous! We must drink to it!"

OF COURSE, the news spread round the parish like wildfire. At least fifty different versions of the story were in circulation by the following morning.

When the banns were called in St. Peter's Church for the first time on Sunday morning, Nona Fitzjames had said pityingly, "I don't know how Melissa let it happen. She won't get Sarne, you know. She doesn't have the position or the style. She can't hope for a better catch than Overberry. Silly child!"

But Melissa, looking radiantly happy, ignored the gossips. "I'm going to be Zoë's chief bridesmaid! Isn't that delightful?"

She seemed so pleased that it was not long before rumours spread to the effect that she was in love with someone else, and that was why she had turned Lord Overberry down. As to who the unknown gentleman was, estimates ranged from Will Kelly the Pedlar, to the Prince Regent.

Arthur was disgusted. "I wonder they didn't add King George to the list. He's a widower now, and at least as suitable as some of the others."

Lucinda glanced across the breakfast table at him. At first she had thought his Monday-morning grumpiness was due to the auction that day. But was it?

THE ATMOSPHERE at the Queen's Head was more festive than businesslike. They were doing a roaring trade in beer, cider and wine. The stables were chock full of horses, and carriages choked the approach lanes.

"Haven't had such a crowd as this in years!" Isaac declared.

It was soon evident that even the largest rooms at the Queen's Head were not sufficiently ample to hold all the bidders. So, since it was a fine, sunny day, Messrs. Challiss and Mowbray moved the auction out into the garden at the rear of the inn.

Mr. Mowbray, who had a voice like a bull, took the chair. He mopped his brow with a large green handkerchief and began to call for bids.

Bellemaine started, offering forty thousand pounds.

Lord Sarne immediately upped that to forty-five thousand.

Sir Kirby Hookmeadow went to forty-five thousand, one hundred pounds.

"Miser!" muttered Arthur.

"Hush!" scolded Lucinda. "That will count as a bid if you're not careful."

It was too late.

"Forty-six thousand!" exclaimed Mr. Mowbray. "Do I hear any advance on forty-six thousand?"

Arthur put his head in his hands and backed out of Mr. Mowbray's sight. It was just as well. Mr. Mowbray had obviously not recognised him.

"Forty-seven thousand!" cried Zoë.

The bidding rose, by a hundred or a thousand pounds at a time. The sun had climbed high when it reached fifty-eight thousand pounds.

"Sixty thousand!" called Bellemaine. "That is my limit. I don't think the place will fetch any more."

Lord Sarne's black eyes gleamed. "It would be a pity to leave it so low. It's undervalued at sixty thousand pounds."

"Do you think so?"

He shrugged. "Sixty-five thousand."

"You are generous, Gabriel!"

An embarrassed flush reddened his tanned countenance. "I can afford it."

"Sixty-five thousand, one hundred pounds," said Sir Kirby Hookmeadow.

Again the bidding proceeded at a snail's pace. The minutes ticked by. The auction had started at ten. It was now nearly noon.

Arthur ground his teeth. "Damme! This is going to take all day!"

"Don't swear, Arthur!" chided Lucinda.

"I can't help it." Arthur grimaced. "I'd like to set their chairs on fire. That would get things hopping!"

Fernand put his hand up to smother a shout of laughter.

"Sixty-eight thousand pounds!" cried Mr. Mowbray and pointed straight at him.

"Oh," gasped Fernand.

"Sixty-eight thousand!" repeated Mr. Mowbray. "Do I hear any rise on sixty-eight thousand? Come, come, ladies and gentlemen! You know very well that Bluebell Manor is worth far more than that! Shall we have seventy thousand? Do I hear seventy thousand?"

Lord Sarne's black eyes caressed Lucinda. "Seventy-five thousand."

Bellemaine looked curiously at him.

"Is something wrong?" enquired Lord Sarne.

"No." She batted her lashes at him. "I am merely surprised. I did not expect that they would get their reserve price."

"Seventy-five thousand, one hundred pounds," Sir Kirby Hookmeadow announced smugly, as if he believed that his would be the highest bid.

Lucinda's heart sank. "Oh, no—not him! *Gabriel, don't let him*."

Dominique's eyes fixed on her and she realized she had said the words aloud.

Pale as an arum lily, Lucinda murmured: "Well . . . he seemed . . . interested. . . ."

"Yes," agreed Dominique.

But in what?

There was a commotion. Mr. Mowbray had suggested that since it was now close to one o'clock, they should break for lunch and resume the bidding in two hours' time.

Sir Kirby was insisting that his was the final bid, that Bluebell Manor should now belong to him.

Mr. Challiss took the stand. "If the bidding is continued after lunch," he asked, "is there anyone who would still be interested in raising the price?"

About fifty hands shot up.

Mr. Challiss and Mr. Mowbray turned to Sir Kirby.

"In that case," concluded Mr. Challiss, "since it is the hour of the midday repast, let us take some refreshment, freely provided by the Earl of Sarne." There was applause. "The bidding will then resume at three this afternoon at seventy-five thousand, one hundred pounds."

The colour flooded back into Lucinda's white face. Automatically, she looked for Lord Sarne. He was not in his chair. She glanced this way and that. Then she saw him riding swiftly toward Sarne Abbey.

Her heart turned to ice.

CHAPTER TWELVE

DAINTY, CRUSTLESS SANDWICHES were being passed around: egg and mayonnaise; salmon and cucumber; beef and mustard. Chicken and mushroom pie was much sought after. Wine flowed. The supply of strawberries and cream was endless. Cheese ramekins came hot from the oven. Scones filled with butter, raspberry jam and clotted cream were favourites.

"Aren't you enjoying the food?" enquired Arthur.

Lucinda glanced at him. "Oh, yes." The strained look did not leave her face. "It is very nice."

"Then why are you frowning?"

"I was wondering what called Gabriel away so suddenly."

"Isn't he here?"

Lucinda shook her head. "I saw him riding back to Sarne Abbey."

"If you wanted to know what called Gabriel away—" Bellemaine's voice was penetratingly clear "—you should have asked me."

"You know?" questioned Arthur.

"Certainly." Bellemaine had a crowd around her now. Not only Arthur and Lord Overberry, but also Melissa, Fernand, Dominique, Zoë and Nona Fitzjames. "A messenger arrived from London. The

Prince Regent requires Gabriel at Carlton House immediately.''

"Why?" Lord Overberry's brows were deeply furrowed.

Bellemaine cast a soulful gaze about her. "Some trouble concerning the Holy Alliance."

Lucinda gnawed her lip. She had heard of the Holy Alliance. It was not, as might be expected, a convocation of religious leaders. Far from it.

The Holy Alliance had been conceived by the Tsar of Russia. Its avowed purpose was to ensure the continuing peace of Europe. But how that could be with Poland wiped off the map, every expression of freedom crushed by force and the Tsar turning covetous eyes toward Turkey, she could not understand. The Prince Regent was not a member. He viewed its dealings with distaste.

"Ah!" mused Zoë. "That explains it."

"How unfortunate that Gabriel should have to rush off like that!" cried Lord Overberry. "And just when he was bidding so well!"

"One cannot keep the Prince Regent waiting upon the outcome of a rustic auction!" declared Nona Fitzjames.

There was an uncomfortable silence.

"Well!" exclaimed Bellemaine gaily. "My bidding is finished, so I shall say farewell, and good luck."

The appropriate acknowledgements were murmured.

"Is anyone coming with me?" asked Bellemaine. "Nona?"

"I should be delighted to accompany you."

As they departed, Lucinda followed them with her eyes. The summons from the Prince Regent had come at an awfully convenient moment, she reflected—for Sir Kirby Hookmeadow. At a stroke, his most powerful rival had been neatly removed. It was highly suspicious.

Oh, stop it! Lucinda chided herself. Sir Kirby would never dare forge such a message! It was no more than an unlucky coincidence!

Her gaze remained on Nona Fitzjames and Bellemaine. Whereas Nona went straight to the carriage, Bellemaine dawdled. It gave Sir Kirby the opportunity to approach her.

What did he want with her? wondered Lucinda. Money? A loan, perhaps? Extra funds so that he could go on bidding? A deep frown disturbed the creamy smoothness of Lucinda's forehead. Bellemaine's words were brief, but it was plain they gave Sir Kirby pleasure. What were they up to?

Then Lucinda smiled and shook her head at her own foolishness. Belle wouldn't help Sir Kirby to win Bluebell Manor! she comforted herself. Not Belle! Never Belle!

The auction was about to resume. Parasols were raised to ward off the heat of the sun. Fans waved gently to stir up a breeze.

Mr. Mowbray mopped his brow with a fresh handkerchief. This one was covered with large blue spots. He mounted the rostrum and announced that the bidding stood at seventy-five thousand, one hundred pounds. He asked if there were any advances.

"Seventy-six thousand!" a country squire boomed.

Again the bidding rose slowly upward a hundred or a thousand pounds at a time, until it reached eighty-six thousand.

"Eighty-six thousand pounds, to Sir Kirby Hookmeadow!" intoned Mr. Mowbray. "Eighty-six thousand once. Eighty-six thousand twice . . ."

"Eighty-seven thousand!" called Zoë.

Sir Kirby Hookmeadow glared at her.

Lucinda heaved a sigh of relief. Her gratitude was expressed in the tremulous smile she gave her friend.

"Eighty-seven thousand pounds!" roared Mr. Mowbray. "I have eighty-seven thousand! Any advance on eighty-seven?"

"Eighty-seven thousand, one hundred pounds," said Sir Kirby Hookmeadow.

"I don't understand it!" grumbled Mr. Bushens. "Sir Kirby doesn't have that kind of capital!"

"Perhaps he borrowed it," suggested his wife.

"No bank would lend him such a sum."

"Not even for Bluebell Manor?"

Mr. Bushens gloomily shook his head. "It's a fine property," he allowed, "but it isn't worth that."

If only Gabriel were here! thought Lucinda as Sir Kirby Hookmeadow raised the price yet again, topping Zoë's new bid of eighty-seven thousand, five hundred.

She put her hand up to massage her throbbing head.

"Eighty-eight thousand pounds!" cried Zoë.

"Eighty-eight thousand, one hundred!" riposted Sir Kirby Hookmeadow.

They tossed the bidding between them until it stood at ninety-four thousand, one hundred.

"Ninety-four thousand, one hundred pounds to Sir Kirby Hookmeadow!" bellowed Mr. Mowbray. "Do I hear any advance on ninety-four thousand one hundred? Ninety-five thousand, anyone?"

Mr. Challiss looked hopefully out over the crowd.

"Ninety-four thousand, one hundred once..." began Mr. Mowbray.

"One hundred thousand!"

It was a shock. The voice was a new one. No one had heard it before. All heads turned. They saw a man who had just arrived at the auction. He was covered in sweat and breathing heavily, as if he had run the whole way.

"Who is he?" The question was on everyone's lips.

They assessed his dress. A plain, pale-grey cloth coat, white cotton shirt, nankeen breeches, dusty old boots. Not the sort of man who would be able to afford such prices. He made his way to an empty chair, then sank down and mopped his brow with a yellow handkerchief.

"Ahem!" Mr. Mowbray cleared his throat. "I have, er, one hundred thousand pounds," he said uncertainly.

"One hundred thousand, one hundred." Sir Kirby Hookmeadow smiled triumphantly. The newcomer could not possibly top that!

His triumph lasted a split second.

The stranger pushed the bid up. "One hundred and five thousand."

"One hundred and five thousand, one hundred," countered Sir Kirby.

"One hundred and ten thousand."

Sir Kirby threw caution to the winds. "One hundred and eleven thousand."

"One hundred and fifteen thousand."

Sir Kirby raised again. But each time he did so, the stranger called a higher bid. As he was forced to fight back, Sir Kirby's face grew redder and redder.

Lucinda held her breath.

How high was this stranger prepared to go?

In the golden afternoon she had her answer.

"One hundred and twenty-five thousand!"

"One hundred and twenty-five thousand pounds! I have one hundred and twenty-five thousand." Mr. Mowbray sounded subdued. "Sir Kirby?"

Sir Kirby, the colour of raw beetroot, shook his head.

"One hundred and twenty-five thousand once! One hundred and twenty-five thousand twice! One hundred and twenty-five thousand three times!" yelled Mr. Mowbray with rising excitement. "One hundred and twenty-five thousand pounds! Bluebell Manor goes to Mr.—er, um . . ."

"Liggatt," supplied the stranger.

"Mr. Liggatt!" The hammer came down with a smart crack on Mr. Mowbray's table. "For one hundred and twenty-five thousand pounds!"

His voice was almost drowned by the cheers that broke out. People rushed to Mr. Liggatt to congratulate him. Chairs were overturned. Men whooped, women screamed. One would have thought Mr. Liggatt had won the war.

It was several minutes before Mr. Challiss and Mr. Mowbray managed to reach Mr. Liggatt's side. One

could see from their serious faces that they were
wondering how on earth such a plainly attired man
was going to pay them. But as he whispered in their
ears, their faces cleared. They brightened, then actually beamed.

Lucinda watched them. What would I give, she
thought, to be able to sit on their shoulders and listen
to what they are saying!

She saw Arthur cross to Mr. Liggatt's side. They
spoke together. They shook hands. When Arthur
returned to her side, he was smiling broadly.

"Good news!" he announced. "Mr. Liggatt does
not want us out until September twenty-first, and he
will take on the servants!"

"That is good news!" agreed Lucinda. "I have been
worried about them."

"Wonderful!" declared Fernand. "And one
hundred and twenty-five thousand pounds! I can
hardly believe it."

"I am so happy for you!" exclaimed Zoë.

"We both are," added Lord Overberry.

"Will you come back to the house with us?" invited Lucinda.

Lord Overberry shook his head. "I'd like to, but…
I'm sorry, Zoë and I are going to London." His arm
was tight round her shoulders. "I want to introduce
her to my family and, of course, to meet hers."

"Well in that case you must not delay," responded
Arthur. "Take Zoë directly to Bluebell Manor. The
servants will pack for her and you can be off at once."

As Zoë and Lord Overberry departed, Arthur remarked, "I would like to have a huge party with all the neighbours...."

"No," interrupted Lucinda.

"No?" Arthur was disappointed.

"We cannot afford it."

"Cannot? But—?"

"We have obligations, Arthur. Especially to the servants. We owe them something for their long years of service. We must clear away our debts. Then, if there is anything left, we can celebrate."

Arthur grimaced. "Ever my practical, realistic sister. I stand corrected." He sighed. "But I would like to celebrate our triumph somehow."

"Why don't you propose to Belle?" teased Lucinda.

He had been saying for years that he was going to, but... He had not been able to propose to Bellemaine Anstruther when she first moved into the district, because they had only just met. He had not been able to propose the year after, because he had to prove himself as a farmer. He had not been able to propose two years ago, because their father had just died. He had not been able to propose last year, because... Lucinda had suggested it.

Arthur gave her an old-fashioned look. Ever since he had admitted his love for Bellemaine to his half sister he had endured her jests.

"Very well," he said suddenly. "I shall."

ARTHUR'S TREAD WAS HEAVY when he returned to Bluebell Manor.

Dominique pursed her lips. "She has refused him."

Fernand clicked his tongue.

A second later, the drawing room doors opened and Arthur came in. His face was grave.

Lucinda's brown eyes were filled with sympathy. "What did Belle say?"

"She turned me down."

"Never mind," comforted Fernand. "Dominique refused me at least ten times before we were married."

Dominique swatted him with her fan.

"It's not her refusal I mind," began Arthur. "Of course, I'm upset, but . . ."

The setting sun played upon Lucinda's face, gilding her camelialike skin. "What happened, Arthur?"

For a long moment Arthur did not reply. When he did speak, his sentences were jerky and uneven. "Belle was getting ready to go out. Her carriage was at the front door. She received me in her drawing room. She sat on the sofa, with that dreadful picture of Admiral Anstruther above her. I don't know whether it was that, or—"

"Yes?" prompted Fernand.

"There was something in her manner. Something strange. Something I couldn't put my finger on. I started to stumble and stutter. I tried to collect myself; to tell her how I had admired her from afar all these years. And she sat there, with the oddest smile upon her face and let me trip over my tongue. . . ." He stopped and took a deep breath to steady himself. "I said how we longed to welcome her into the family and I asked her to be my wife, and—and she laughed."

Lucinda had her back to the window. The dying rays of the afternoon sun made her hair seem almost golden. "That does not sound like Belle!"

"No. It doesn't. I was quite shaken."

"My poor pet!" exclaimed Dominique.

"She—she said she was sorry she had to decline my proposal," continued Arthur numbly. "She said she was sure that you, Lucinda, would regret that more than I did."

Lucinda gasped and shook her head in denial.

"Then," concluded Arthur, "she excused herself, saying she had a prior engagement. So of course, I left."

"How very odd!" declared Lucinda.

"It is more than odd," stated Fernand grimly. "It is . . . unbecoming in a lady."

IT WAS THURSDAY when Lucinda's accounts were finally settled. The last bill had been paid, the last sum of money set aside for bonuses.

Lucinda put her account books away. With Arthur, Fernand and Dominique, she threw a party for the servants. It was a lighthearted affair, with dancing on the lawn. There were masses of cakes and sausages. A sword-swallower came from a nearby circus and an itinerant juggler appeared, along with a clown.

They served homemade cider. And woe to the uninitiated who poured it down their throats. It was strong enough to knock out Goliath!

THAT EVENING Fernand remarked, "I think we must be going."

"Must you really?" asked Lucinda.

"If our son is to be born at Château Niverne we must return to France tomorrow."

"Our *son*?" countered Dominique. "You realize it could be a daughter."

"With you, *ma chère*, I should not be surprised if it were twins. Or triplets. Or quadruplets."

"What is that supposed to mean?"

"Merely that you are the most awkward woman I have ever known. The most obstinate. The most difficult—"

"How dare you?" Dominique was bristling with fury. "You pigheaded son of a race of spendthrift degenerates! Insult me, will you? I'll have my child born here in England, I tell you!"

"You will do no such thing!"

"That's what you think!"

"Dominique, it is my wish..." Fernand began pompously.

Lucinda and Arthur had been through many of these little misunderstandings. A knowing look passed between them. Together they rose and discreetly left the room.

THE NEXT MORNING, Arthur took the lovebirds by the gentlest, least bumpy route to Weymouth, whence they proposed to sail to Brittany and the Château Niverne.

Lucinda did not go with them. At the last moment there had been a message from Messrs. Challiss and Mowbray indicating there were a few details to be settled regarding the estate.

Since Arthur knew the best route to Weymouth, and since Lucinda was capable of dealing with the trouble, it was decided that she should remain behind.

To Lucinda's surprise, the business did not take as long as had been anticipated. It was still morning when she rode back home.

Was it worthwhile setting out after the others? she wondered. Considering they were travelling slowly, and in a landau, while she would be riding, it was possible she could catch them up.

The sound of carriage wheels approaching from behind a broad hedge made Lucinda draw Pearl up. She waited. Presently Nona Fitzjames's moss-green barouche, drawn by six high-stepping white horses, came into view.

Nona, with a puce muslin pelisse over her ivory morning dress, reclined against the dark brown leather seat, fanning herself as if she were in a great fever. Bellemaine sat beside her, twirling a buttercup-yellow parasol.

"Good morning!" Lucinda greeted them.

"Good morning!" replied Nona Fitzjames.

"Good morning!" Bellemaine signaled the coachman to advance. Nona Fitzjames countermanded the order.

The barouche, which had moved forward two feet, stopped. And there it sat, completely blocking Lucinda's path.

"Lovely day, isn't it?" asked Nona.

"Delightful," agreed Lucinda. Through the veil of her bronze lashes, she was studying Bellemaine. She could not think of her the way she used to. Bellemaine's cruel rejection of Arthur's proposal had changed things between them. Lucinda now saw her in a different light. Unbidden, her mind went back over a host of little incidents, reviewing them and revising her opinion of Bellemaine still more.

Suddenly Lucinda realized that Nona was in the middle of describing her own and Bellemaine's visit to London.

"...and the summons from the Prince Regent was a hoax!" Nona Fitzjames almost spat the word. "Some wretched jester tricked Gabriel!"

Lucinda gasped. Sir Kirby had dared—or had it been Bellemaine?

"He must have been annoyed," she murmured.

"He was at first. It was a bad business. A very bad business. So embarrassing." Nona tapped her fan crossly. "Then something really did come up."

"Indeed?"

"I don't know precisely what. A diplomatic affair. Very secret. Gabriel went to Carlton House to attend to it. The Prince Regent kindly invited us to join him—"

"But you did not?"

"No." Nona halted briefly. "There was no point. Gabriel and His Royal Highness were completely involved in whatever it was. Every moment of their time was occupied. We should not have seen them, not even for a second. So we felt it would be better if we returned to Dorset."

"Very wise," commented Lucinda.

"We are on our way to Sarne Abbey," said Belle-maine meaningfully. "We shall wait for Gabriel there."

All at once Lucinda understood the significance of Bellemaine's remarks to Arthur.

She is telling me we are rivals! realized Lucinda.

The colour fled from her cheeks.

"I—I hope you both have a—a pleasant stay," managed Lucinda.

"I am sure we shall," replied Nona Fitzjames. "Sarne Abbey is charming in the summer. Truly at its best."

"You have stayed there before?"

"Many times. As a member of the family, I can come and go whenever I please."

"A rare privilege."

"Yes, indeed. Naturally, I don't impose...."

"Naturally."

"...but I thought," continued Nona, "that in the circumstances, Gabriel would not mind our coming."

Suddenly, Bellemaine's words returned to haunt Lucinda. *Nona Fitzjames commented that Gabriel and I were destined for each other.* A cold chill swept over her.

Bellemaine and Sir Kirby, she thought. *He wants Bluebell Manor—and me. She wants Gabriel.* So they joined forces. Belle must have lent Sir Kirby money to bid with at the auction!

A grim smile crossed Lucinda's lips. I wonder how she'll take it when she learns he failed!

Her smile faded as Nona Fitzjames prattled on, "There is no telling when Gabriel will be back, you

see. It may be a matter of a few hours, or a few days.
And I felt that in view of what has passed, he would
wish us to be there. Waiting.''

Waiting? Lucinda asked herself silently. *Waiting for
what?*

Idly, Bellemaine touched the fourth finger of her
left hand. It was almost as if she had heard Lucinda's
unspoken question, almost as if she answered aloud.

For Gabriel to propose to me, *of course!*

CHAPTER THIRTEEN

THE BAROUCHE REMAINED where it was, still blocking Lucinda's way. Lucinda itched to make it move. It was with an effort that she maintained her air of unconcern.

Bellemaine fidgeted with the jewelled watch that hung on a gold chain around her neck. "Have you seen much of Sir Kirby since the auction?"

Lucinda's brown eyes narrowed. Her cheeks burned. "No. Should I have?"

"Well, since he bought the place..."

"You are out of touch, Belle. Sir Kirby did not buy Bluebell Manor."

Bellemaine frowned. "But I understood he would."

"He couldn't meet the price."

"What was the price?"

"One hundred and twenty-five thousand pounds."

Bellemaine's mouth fell open.

"One hundred and twenty-five thousand!" gasped Nona Fitzjames. "But that is far more than the property is worth. Whoever paid it must have taken leave of his senses!"

"The buyer won't thank you for saying so," observed Lucinda tartly.

"And who is the buyer?" Bellemaine wanted to know.

"A gentleman by the name of Liggatt," answered Lucinda. "Mr. Richard Liggatt."

"Liggatt. Liggatt. I've heard the name before," Nona said. "I can't think where!"

"I have never heard it," complained Bellemaine. "Who is he? Who were his parents? What is his fortune?"

"I'm afraid I know nothing about him," returned Lucinda. "Perhaps Messrs. Challiss and Mowbray will be able to tell you. And now—" she addressed Nona Fitzjames "—if you will excuse me?"

"Certainly," responded the older woman.

The coachman moved the barouche forward. Lucinda edged Pearl around the back of it. As she galloped away, her blue riding habit fluttering in the breeze, Nona Fitzjames exclaimed, "Ah, I have it! I know where I have heard the name Liggatt."

Bellemaine sighed wearily. "Where?" she asked in bored tones.

"He is the chap Gabriel took with him to Oxford."

Bellemaine stiffened. She glanced at Lucinda to see if the latter could have heard. But Lucinda was out of earshot. Indeed, she was almost out of sight.

"Took to Oxford?"

"Yes. Richard Liggatt is terribly clever," explained Nona Fitzjames, "but very poor. In return for his education, he, er, looked after Gabriel, shall we say."

"Looked after?"

"Cleaned his boots for him. Fetched and carried things. Helped him when he got into scrapes."

"Oh."

"It worked out very well. They both received honours degrees. But I can't remember what happened to Liggatt after that."

Bellemaine caressed her jewelled watch. "How very interesting, Nona. You know a surprising lot about people in these parts."

"I've lived here all my life; I should do."

"Do you suppose Mr. Richard Liggatt is clever enough to have earned . . . that amount of money?"

"I cannot say. He might be."

"Or might not be," muttered Bellemaine reflectively. "He could have been acting as someone's agent. And if the real buyer is—I shall have to work fast!"

"Eh? What was that?" barked Nona Fitzjames.

"I must not shirk my duty to Sir Kirby. While I am at Sarne Abbey I must call upon him."

"Certainly." Nona Fitzjames suspected nothing.

Bellemaine smiled.

WHEN LUCINDA RETURNED to Bluebell Manor, she found Melissa pacing up and down, wearing a hole in the drawing room carpet.

"Melissa! What brings you here?"

Melissa grimaced. "Where is Arthur?"

Lucinda stared at her friend. "He has taken Dominique and Fernand to Weymouth."

"How *could* he? Now all is lost."

"I beg your pardon?"

"He should have been here!" Melissa sat down abruptly and rested her chin on her hands. "Why, today of all days, did he have to go to Weymouth?"

Lucinda took the chair opposite her friend. She removed her tan riding gloves.

"Why shouldn't Arthur go to Weymouth?"

"Because I'm in a dreadful pickle, and only he can get me out of it!"

"What kind of a pickle?"

"I overheard Mama and Papa discussing my future."

"And?"

"Now they want me to marry Sir Kirby Hook-meadow."

"Surely you are joking!"

"I am not joking. Furthermore, they don't intend to let me say no. They say I have a reputation for fickleness."

"So you have."

Lord Overberry was not the only titled personage whose offer of marriage Melissa had turned down.

Melissa sighed in exasperation. "What else can I do? I can't marry without love! Oh, if only—"

"Yes?"

"I wish my parents didn't insist on my marrying someone who is titled."

"There is nothing wrong with that, is there?"

"Yes, there is."

Lucinda surveyed her friend. Melissa was wearing a sprigged muslin dress, its high waist emphasized by a green satin sash, its scalloped border revealing her dainty ankles. An emerald necklace gleamed at her throat, and emerald earrings set off her tiny ears.

The whole ensemble was quite incorrect for a casual morning drive. But for a special occasion, such as the

announcement of an engagement... *She told me I was
the only man in the world for her,* Lucinda seemed to
hear Arthur relating. *She wasn't herself! She didn't
know what she was saying!* Lucinda's brown eyes
widened as the light slowly dawned. "You mean...?"

"Yes," said Melissa. "I mean I'm in love with
Arthur. Your brother! I want to marry him. And the
wretch won't propose. I could cheerfully box his
ears."

Lucinda laughed.

"It's not funny!"

"Poor Arthur! He is so blinkered where you are
concerned, Melissa. He sees you as a sister. You will
have to open his eyes!"

Melissa became very thoughtful. "Thank you,
Lucinda. You have been a great help."

Lucinda was standing by the window watching
Melissa's caned whisky being driven at a fine clip
down the road when Hebe's discreet cough made her
turn her head. "Will you be going to Weymouth today, Miss Edrington?"

Lucinda considered for a moment. "No," she decided. "I think not."

LUCINDA SPENT a peaceful evening at the pianoforte,
enthusiastically playing her favourite tunes and hitting
every single wrong note with gay abandon.

She was about to retire when she caught the sound
of carriage wheels on the gravel drive. "That is probably Arthur," she informed her maid. "Let him in,
please, Hebe."

Hebe unbolted the door. It was pushed roughly aside. The maid went sprawling onto the floor. She screamed. She covered her head with her apron. Lucinda stared, appalled.

There in the doorway was Mr. Bushens, pale, disheveled and brandishing a brace of pistols.

"Where is the young whippersnapper!" he roared. "What has he done with my daughter! If he doesn't hand her over this instant I'll have him horsewhipped!"

Lucinda drew herself up to her full height. "What is the meaning of this unseemly intrusion?"

Mr. Bushens gaped at her as if he had never seen her before. He waved the guns uncertainly. "You—you—you are in league with him!"

"I don't know what you are talking about." Lucinda hoped he did not realize that she was frightened out of her wits. "Hebe, please summon the footmen and have Mr. Bushens ejected. He is plainly drunk."

Hebe emerged cautiously from behind her apron.

Mr. Bushens was glaring at Lucinda. She met his stare with her own stonily imperious one. His eyes wavered and dropped before it.

"I—I am sorry. That was...uncalled for."

Lucinda gave a brief nod in acknowledgement. "Hebe, take the pistols from Mr. Bushens, if you please."

Hebe seized the pistols from Mr. Bushens's unresisting hands.

"Perhaps—" the regal air was easier for Lucinda to maintain now that he was disarmed "—you would care to come into the drawing room and tell me what this is all about?''

A few minutes later Mr. Bushens sat with his head in his hands, weeping. ''Melissa s-said she was c-coming here...''

''She did come here,'' admitted Lucinda.

''She—and Arthur...''

''Arthur was not here when Melissa came. Only I was here.''

Mr. Bushens gobbled.

''I was alone,'' Lucinda reaffirmed.

Mr. Bushens sniffed into a fine linen handkerchief. ''Mrs. Bushens and I have always wanted only what is best for Melissa.''

''Of course.''

''She is heiress to a considerable fortune. She should marry someone who is titled. It is only right and proper.''

''She does not want to. She told me that.''

''She told us, too.'' He sighed. ''She left a note which her mother found after she had gone. She said the only man she had ever loved was Arthur, and if she could not have him, she would have no one.''

''And you find my brother is unsuitable?''

Mr. Bushens was embarrassed. ''He—well, he...''

''Mrs. Bushens!'' announced Hebe.

Pale as the ghost of Lady Macbeth, Mrs. Bushens strode in. ''Where are they?''

Lucinda lifted her shoulders gracefully. ''If you mean Melissa and Arthur, they are probably in Weymouth.''

''Weymouth!'' Mrs. Bushens was astounded.

"Arthur took Dominique and Fernand to Weymouth this morning," explained Lucinda kindly. "They were intending to sail from there to France. I told Melissa that. From what Mr. Bushens has said, I think—but of course I am not certain—that she went there also."

"I see." Mrs. Bushens glared fiercely at her husband and Lucinda in turn, while she decided on the proper course of action. "In that case, Lucinda, I feel we have trespassed upon your hospitality enough. We shall search for Melissa in Weymouth."

As the Bushens's carriage rumbled south, Lucinda heaved a sigh of relief. *And now*, she thought, *I shall be able to sleep.* It was not to be.

Fernand turned up next, and Lucinda received him *en déshabillé*, with her cinnamon curls tumbling free. Fernand, in a fine fury, pushed her into the drawing room.

Lucinda's sleepy eyes widened. "Fernand, what has happened?"

"Everything!" raged Fernand. "Arthur is a fool. A blind fool."

"Yes, of course he is. Where is Dominique?"

"In our hotel in Weymouth. She will not stir hand nor foot until she finds out where Arthur and Melissa have gone!"

"Gone?"

"Aren't they here?"

"No." Lucinda wrapped a rug round her legs and draped a shawl over her shoulders. "I'm cold!" she said pointedly.

Fernand, cursing violently, lit the fire.

"You did not meet the Bushens, I take it."

Fernand gazed at her in pure astonishment. "Why on earth should I meet the Bushens?"

"Because they were looking for Melissa and Arthur, too. I sent them to Weymouth about"—she paused to glance at the gilded carriage clock which rested on the mantelpiece"—two hours ago."

Fernand snorted. "No. I did not meet them. They must have gone by the other road." He threw himself into the chair opposite Lucinda and sipped his brandy. "I suppose you would like to know what happened?"

Lucinda nodded.

"Melissa arrived in Weymouth just as Dominique and I were about to board the only ship departing for France today. She rushed to the captain, wild-eyed, demanding passage. He told her he could not take anyone else. And what do you think she did then?"

"I can't imagine."

"She fainted—right into Arthur's arms!"

Lucinda felt an uncontrollable urge to giggle. She bit into her handkerchief to stop it.

"And when she opened her big blue eyes, can you guess what she said?" growled Fernand crossly.

Lucinda, her handkerchief still tightly between her teeth, shook her head.

"She said that her life in England has become intolerable and she was fleeing the country, never to return!"

"Sh-she d-didn't!" stuttered Lucinda. "Melissa wouldn't! She couldn't!"

"Hah!" snarled Fernand. "Much you know about it! Dominique, being practical, asked her whether she had any money or anywhere to stay—"

"And she hadn't?" Lucinda had seen no sign of a reticule or any baggage when Melissa had called.

"No," Fernand confirmed. "Dominique then asked her what she would do if she did get passage to the Continent. Had she funds abroad?"

"And again she said no?"

"Worse! She said she would rather work as a kitchen maid than be forced to give herself in marriage to Sir Kirby Hookmeadow!"

CHAPTER FOURTEEN

LUCINDA COULD NO LONGER contain herself. The handkerchief was whipped away from her face. She laughed aloud.

"It is not amusing!" declared Fernand. "It is disgraceful. That a well-bred young lady should even *think* such a thing..."

"Yes." Lucinda tried to look contrite. "It is really quite, quite dreadful."

"Naturally, Dominique and I remonstrated with her." Fernand stood up and warmed his back by the fire. "We reminded her of the scandal, of the shame, of how her parents would suffer. We pointed out that ladies in her position do not lower themselves—"

"And then?" interrupted Lucinda.

"She wept!"

"Melissa wept?"

"Isn't that what I have just said?" Fernand gnashed his teeth. "It was most touching, most affecting. She does it even better now than she did when we were children. Do you remember how she used to let great tears run down her cheeks whenever we asked her?"

"I remember." The handkerchief was hastily replaced. Lucinda's cinnamon curls danced as she shook with silent laughter.

"Well, Arthur didn't!" Fernand flung himself back into his chair. "He wouldn't listen to me! I told him it was an act. He insisted it was not. The idiot! The lunatic!"

Lucinda crushed the handkerchief in her fingers. "What did he do?"

"He declared that Melissa was unwell and that she had to have a room in a hotel where she could lie down and recover. And Dominique agreed!"

"You did not?"

"I thought—I still think—her parents ought to have been summoned!"

"And what then? A hasty marriage to Sir Kirby Hookmeadow? You cannot be serious, Fernand!"

"There are other suitable prospects."

"And Melissa has refused every single one of them."

"What! Why?"

"She wants Arthur."

"You knew?"

"Not at first. I saw signs, but..." Lucinda lifted her shoulders. "I wasn't absolutely certain until Melissa told me herself. Today. Or is it yesterday, now?"

Fernand muttered something venomous about *les femmes*.

Lucinda ignored it. "What happened then?"

"Dominique and I went ahead with our preparations to sail." He paused and glowered at the flames dancing cheerfully in the grate. "The next thing I knew Arthur had vanished. And so had Melissa."

"Without trace?"

Fernand nodded grimly. "Dominique refused to sail. She just got off the ship, sat down on her hatbox and refused to budge until she knew what had happened to them."

"So you disembarked."

"I was forced to!" Smouldering, Fernand drank some more brandy. "We found out that Melissa had pawned her emerald necklace and earrings."

"They must have fetched a pretty penny!"

"More than a thousand pounds."

"In that case, Fernand, I don't think you need worry. She will travel in comfort to her destination."

Fernand leaned forward. "Lucinda, do you understand nothing? Melissa is unchaperoned. Think of the scandal, the disgrace!" He pressed his lips tightly together. "I had hoped Melissa would come here. Or Arthur. Or both. Then things could have been fixed . . . no one need have known . . . But they are not here! And since they have *both* disappeared, rumours will start! Have you no idea of the damage—"

Lucinda yawned. "Fernand, Arthur may be a fool, but he is not a cad. He'll see to it that he and Melissa are married."

Fernand paled. "Do you—do you mean—they have eloped?"

Lucinda shrugged.

Fernand uttered an oath. "*I* have been a fool!"

"Yes, Fernand," agreed Lucinda complacently.

Fernand hardly heard her. "I should have guessed. They are in love. Bah! They have gone to Gretna Green!" And then, before she could stop him, he declared, "I am going after them!"

At last, thought Lucinda, I may be able to sleep.
She was wrong again.

AT DAWN a loud thumping on the door awakened half
the household. Lucinda was one of the unlucky ones.

Mr. and Mrs. Bushens stood on the doorstep.

"They are not in Weymouth!" intoned Mr. Bushens.

"I know." Lucinda stifled a yawn. "My brother
Fernand came after you had gone."

"We passed no one on the road."

"You must have gone by another route," responded Lucinda sleepily. "Fernand told me they were
not in Weymouth." She stifled another yawn.
"Melissa has pawned her jewels."

Mr. and Mrs. Bushens exchanged glances.

"Er, what else did you learn?" enquired Mrs.
Bushens.

"Nothing, really." Lucinda smothered an incipient
yawn. "Fernand thinks they have gone to Gretna
Green."

"Aaah!" screamed Mrs. Bushens. "We must stop
them!"

"But—" began Lucinda.

They were not listening. They hurtled back to their
carriage. Within seconds they were driving away,
exhorting the coachman to go "Faster! Faster!"

"But they may not have gone to Gretna Green!"
Lucinda called out after them. Then the carriage
lamps disappeared from view and Lucinda sighed.

"Would you like me to pursue them, Miss Edrington?" asked Yarr.

Lucinda turned.

The butler was wearing a long white nightshirt. A blue nightcap sat on his grey hair, with a tassel that dangled onto his right shoulder. His feet were encased in large, floppy slippers. A steadily burning candle was in his left hand.

"Er, no, I think not," replied Lucinda. "Thank you, Yarr. But the Bushens have fast horses. None of us could catch them."

THE FOLLOWING WEEK passed peacefully.

There was no news for eight whole days from either Arthur or Melissa. Nor was there a peep out of any of the others.

Before breakfast on Sunday, Lucinda put on a white crepe dress with a thin gold belt around the waist. It had a high neck, with a standing ruff, pinked at the edges. Over her Honiton lace mobcap, she placed a straw bonnet, covered with pink flowers, and tied under her chin with a pink satin ribbon.

She took her place in Saint Peter's Church as usual. The Reverend John Isbister was preaching his early-morning sermon. He had chosen to speak on the duty of children to their parents, and in particular on the impropriety of marrying without one's parents' blessing. He especially stressed the inadvisability of assisting in elopements. All the while, people kept gazing accusingly at Lucinda.

She bore it for about ten minutes. Then she got up, glanced contemptuously over the congregation and swept out. Behind her, she could hear people muttering; "Brazen hussy!" Her cheeks flamed with anger. She did not give them the satisfaction of looking back.

Once outside in the warm sunshine, Lucinda took a deep breath to steady her nerves. Then suddenly, she realized she was no longer alone. She turned her head. There, in a showy gauze dress that was a riot of colour, with a fine Leghorn bonnet to match, was Bellemaine.

"Good morning. I thought I saw you coming out of church."

"Good morning," replied Lucinda. "Yes, I left early."

Bellemaine's manner was easy and natural—as it had used to be. Yet Lucinda was on her guard. What was she up to? she wondered.

"I am surprised you went in the first place."

"Why?"

"I wouldn't have been brave enough to go to church after what has happened."

"To what are you referring, Belle?"

"Arthur and Melissa's elopement, of course. It is the talk of the county."

Lucinda was silent.

"There is a rumour," Bellemaine went on, "that the Bushens will charge Arthur with kidnapping an heiress."

Lucinda went ramrod stiff. Her finely pencilled tawny eyebrows arched. "Arthur and Melissa are of age. If they have eloped, they have done so entirely of their own free will."

"I can't tell you how glad I am to hear that. Kidnapping is such a beastly crime. Prison wouldn't agree with Arthur—or you, come to that."

Lucinda cast her eyes down to hide the anger smouldering in them.

"Such a handicap could, er, ruin a lady's chances of marriage."

Lucinda pressed her hands together. "There has been no kidnapping."

"Ah! Well, they do say that it is always those most closely involved in a tragedy who are the last to learn of it. And it is certainly true in your case, Lucinda."

"Since Arthur has done nothing wrong, and neither have I, there can be no tragedy. Melissa—"

Bellemaine laughed merrily. "Oh, I wasn't talking about *that* my dear!"

"Weren't you?"

"Dear me, no. I was referring to another member of your family—your mother."

"Indeed?"

"You didn't know, did you, that your parents neglected to get married."

CHAPTER FIFTEEN

LUCINDA WENT WHITE. "That remark is in very poor taste, Belle!"

Bellemaine shrugged. "Sir Kirby and I were discussing you only the other day. He could not recall, though he has lived in this county many years, when your parents were married. So we went to Saint Peter's and had a look in the register. There was no record of their marrying."

Lucinda did not answer. Despite the warmth of the sun, she seemed to feel ice coursing through her veins.

"It would be dreadful if such a thing were to become known," stated Bellemaine.

Still Lucinda made no comment.

"If you were to marry a respectable gentleman, however—a knight, say," continued Bellemaine, "it would not have to come out."

Lucinda's brown eyes narrowed with puzzlement and suspicion.

"Sir Kirby and I would guarantee that."

The light dawned. "You are telling me to marry Sir Kirby?" A month ago, Lucinda would not have thought Bellemaine was capable of such treachery.

"I wouldn't dream of telling you to do any such thing. I was merely pointing out the advantages of ac cepting a proposal of marriage from a man like Sir Kirby." Even as Bellemaine spoke, the church doors opened and the congregation started to stream out. "Consider it."

Abruptly, she left Lucinda and went in search of Nona Fitzjames.

Lucinda walked through the churchyard. Her mind was in turmoil. Her usually clear countenance wore a shadow.

"It's not true!" she muttered. "Belle is lying—she must be!"

Would her mother, the dignified, graceful French Marquise de Niverne have lived unmarried with an English gentleman for more than twenty years?

Hidden from view by the high tombstones and a spreading oak tree, Lucinda waited impatiently until finally the last person left the church. Then she found the verger. Soon she was combing through the heavy leather-bound volumes of the Parish Register which was in his charge.

It did not take Lucinda long. She found her father's baptism and her Uncle Cerdic's baptism. She found her father's marriage to Hester Warton. She found Arthur's baptism. She found the death of Hester Warton Edrington. She found a notice of her own baptism: "Lucinda, daughter of Edgar Edrington, Gentleman, and his Wife, Clotilde."

But try as she might, she could not find the confirmation of their marriage. Bellemaine's accusation seared her soul. Were her parents married?

Lucinda closed the volumes. It was no use asking the Reverend John Isbister. He had not been in the

Parish above two years. Dear, kind, muddleheaded The Reverend Augustus Merryweather would have known. But he, alas, was with his Maker.

If only there were some other kind of proof of the marriage—a certificate of marriage for instance. Lucinda sighed. Such things did exist, but they were rare. Most people relied on witnesses. In close-knit communities there was no need for more.

Disconsolately, Lucinda walked from the vestry down the path to her carriage. Sir Kirby Hookmeadow was waiting for her.

"Have you come to your senses, Lucinda?"

"I am not sure I understand you, Sir Kirby."

"Did Belle not speak to you? Did she not tell you that I still wish to marry you?"

"She mentioned it."

"She impressed upon you the—ahem!—necessity for considering my proposal?"

Lucinda's nostrils flared.

"You are silent," stated Sir Kirby. "Perhaps you don't realize..."

Lucinda studied the grass-edged path at her feet.

Sir Kirby decided to be blunt. "I gather you were looking for proof of your parents' marriage. It isn't here. It isn't in the chapel at Sarne Abbey, either. I have looked. And there is no record of your parents' marriage anywhere in the whole of Dorset."

Lucinda glared at him as he went on, "If your parents were not married, if you are illegitimate..." Sir Kirby studied her to see if she understood.

She did, and her cheeks burned with shame. She would be an outcast, she realized. It was not only the fact of her illegitimacy, but the long concealment of it which would damn her. Her friends, her neighbours, even her relations would turn their backs on her. She would have to leave Dorset—England even—forever.

She pictured her life as an exile, wandering from city to city, country to country, deserted, miserable, alone. She shuddered. She would be pitied, she mused, but never accepted.

"I . . ." she began.

"Before you speak, hear me out!" Sir Kirby leered at her. "The, er, omission need not become known. You can go on living as a respectable lady. *My* lady."

Lucinda's hands clenched so tightly that her fingernails dug into her palms.

"What? Not a word! You don't even ask me my terms?"

"What . . . are your . . . terms?"

Sir Kirby looked smugly satisfied. "It is that your dowry shall be your share of Bluebell Manor."

Lucinda frowned. "But it has already been sold!"

"Tut-tut. You are too nice about it. The buyer will certainly acquiesce. The land which I shall offer in exchange will be more than ample recompense."

Lucinda blinked in astonishment.

Why is my half of Bluebell Manor so important to him? she wondered. Aloud, she said, "It is impossible. My land has already been sold. I cannot take it back now."

"I think you can. Ladies are known for their fickleness. And your reputation, your future happiness, both demand a change of heart!"

Lucinda's brown eyes blazed. "Never!"

Sir Kirby bowed and replaced his hat. "You know where to find me when you have, er, regained your composure."

Lucinda's expression as she watched Sir Kirby depart was a mixture of loathing and fear. Bellemaine was right! No record of her parents' marriage existed in Saint Peter's. But was Sir Kirby telling the truth when he said there was nothing at Sarne Abbey nor in the rest of Dorset?

Lucinda was so lost in her reverie that she did not notice a horseman approaching at great speed, on a powerful stallion which gleamed with sweat. She wasn't aware of him until he jumped down and stood before her, until she sniffed the scent of his body and heard him say, "Lucinda! I hoped I might find you here!"

Then Lucinda found herself looking directly into the Earl of Sarne's brilliant black eyes.

His inky hair had been swept into disarray by the wind. His chestnut coat was undone. His shirt was open, revealing his bronzed skin.

He grinned ruefully. "I know. I'm a sight." His mouth quirked suddenly with good humour. "I rode here after Arthur and Melissa's wedding."

Lucinda's legs gave way beneath her. If there had not been a low stone wall just behind her, she would have sat down on the path, so great was her astonishment.

"They are m-married?"

"Yes. In Canterbury. By special licence. I witnessed it."

The Bushens will charge Arthur with kidnapping an heiress, Lucinda seemed to hear Bellemaine suggesting.

"Oh, no!" groaned Lucinda. A charge of kidnapping! Lord Sarne involved!

"What's the matter?" The light faded from his eyes. "You do not disapprove, surely?" All at once he smiled, a dazzling, warm smile, guaranteed to melt any heart. "I must tell you that I, for one, will be very pleased to have Melissa as my sister-in-law."

Lucinda stared at him.

He dropped on one knee beside her. "Do you not understand, Lucinda?" He was serious now. "I am asking you to marry me. To be my wife."

Lucinda's lips parted.

Bellemaine's cruel words came back to haunt her. *Perhaps you are unaware of the fact that your parents neglected to get married.*

She could not tell him. She dared not accept his proposal.

"I cannot marry you, Gabriel." The words came slowly. To her ears, they sounded like the tolling of a death knell.

Lord Sarne's black brows drew together. "Cannot? Why?"

Lucinda was silent.

His hands gripped her arms just above her wrists. She struggled briefly, like a bird caught in a snare. But

the pressure increased and she realized it was useless
to fight him.

"You cannot marry me?" he demanded again.
"Why?" His eyes searched her face. He tried to read
the answer in her soul. "Do I repel you? Am I disgusting to you? Is there someone else?"

"No. Of course not." She spoke hurriedly, hiding
her eyes with her lashes. Her body jerked like a
puppet's on a string.

Lord Sarne looked at her hands, imprisoned in his.
He did not release her. His voice became dangerously
quiet. "You find me amusing? A figure of fun, perhaps? It was not love I thought I had found, but
mockery. When you first saw me, you laughed at me.
And you have been laughing ever since, haven't you?"

There was no reply.

His voice became even more savage and raw. "Did
you enjoy playing with me? Was it fun to set me free
and then capture me all over again? Did it give you
pleasure?"

He stopped speaking abruptly. His hands were wet.
His head went up. Tears were falling from her eyes and
splashing onto his fingers like raindrops.

"Don't!" His voice had dropped to a hoarse whisper. His hands caressed her cheek. "Don't cry, Lucinda!"

For a moment their eyes met and he saw a profound anguish in hers.

"What is it?" he enquired anxiously.

Her mouth trembled.

"Tell me!"

She shook her head.

He tried to take her in his arms, but she tore free and ran to her carriage. He watched her until she had vanished from view. She did not turn round once. If she had, she would have seen him gazing after her, his eyes revealing a mixture of pain, bewilderment and desire which was tearing him apart.

"LUCINDA, DEAREST!" Zoë Joliffe was back. Exuberantly, she flung her arms around her friend.

Lucinda shrank from her.

"Whatever is the matter?" asked Zoë. "Have I come at the wrong time?"

Lucinda shook her head. "I—I was just surprised. I didn't expect to find you here."

"That's obvious!" Zoë's blue gingham gown swished as she dropped into a chair. She studied Lucinda's ashen cheeks and her red-rimmed eyes. "There is something wrong, isn't there?"

Lucinda shut the door behind her.

Wrong? Wrong was hardly the word for it. Disastrous would have been better.

She made a little gesture of despair. "Tell me your news first, and then I shall tell you mine. How was London? How did Vincent's family receive you?"

"We had a wonderful visit in London. Vincent's family adore me; and my family adore him. We also went to Canterbury, where"—she paused for effect "—Vincent and I were witnesses at Melissa's and Arthur's wedding."

"I know."

Zoë frowned. "You know?"

"I met Gabriel. He told me Melissa and Arthur were married."

"Well, aren't you pleased?"

"Pleased!" countered Lucinda angrily. "When Arthur may face a charge of kidnapping an heiress? When we could be dragged through the courts like common criminals? *Pleased!*"

"What are you talking about?"

"It is customary when a wealthy woman elopes that her parents lay charges of kidnapping an heiress. Mr. and Mrs. Bushens—"

"Oh, Lucinda!" interrupted Zoë. "Who has been feeding you all this nonsense?"

"There was a mention—"

"Bah! There will be no kidnapping charges! Melissa is much too clever for that! In fact," added Zoë thoughtfully, "I didn't realize that under those fluffy blond curls, she actually does have a brain."

Lucinda snorted.

"Melissa pawned her emerald necklace and earrings," resumed Zoë. "With the money she raised, she paid for the elopement herself. She even persuaded the Archbishop to grant her a special licence. And you should have seen what it cost her! Believe me, nobody could charge Arthur with kidnapping her."

Lucinda gaped. "You mean . . . it's all right?"

"Of course it's all right! Did you really think that Vincent and I—and Gabriel, too—would have been witnesses at the wedding if we thought were going to be charged as accessories to a kidnapping?"

Lucinda gnawed her lip.

"If anyone was kidnapped," concluded Zoë, "it was Arthur. Melissa fairly dragged him to the altar. No, truly."

Lucinda was laughing.

"That's better. You gave me a fright when you first came in. You were so deathly white I thought something must be desperately wrong."

Slowly, Lucinda undid her bonnet and put it down on the table between them. With great care she adjusted her mobcap, so that her hair framed her face.

Zoë watched her closely. "Something *is* desperately wrong, isn't it?"

"Whatever makes you say that?" Lucinda was artificially bright.

Zoë put her head on one side. "Vincent said he thought Gabriel was going to propose to you. Did he?"

Lucinda's brown eyes were firmly fastened on the claw-footed legs of the table. "Yes."

"You didn't accept?"

"I . . ." Nervously she licked her lips. "I couldn't . . . accept."

Zoë leaned forward across the table, so that her long nose almost touched Lucinda's snub one. "Why not?"

"I couldn't bear to—to disgrace him."

"I beg your pardon?"

Lucinda twisted her slender hands this way and that. At last she spoke. "Belle told me that my parents were . . . not married."

"What! But—" Zoë sat bolt upright.

Lucinda silenced her with a wave of her hand. "I looked for the entry of their marriage in the Parish

Register. It was not there. I—I was leaving when Gabriel came." She swallowed. "You know what it means if my parents were not married. You know what I would be. I can't marry him. I couldn't bear to drag him down, to dishonour his name...."

"Lucinda! I cannot be hearing aright!" Zoë thumped her ears.

"My parents were not married in Saint Peter's Church, nor, I believe, in the Chapel at Sarne Abbey, nor, it seems, anywhere in Dorset."

"Then they must have got married somewhere else!"

"You sound very sure."

"Of course I am sure! Your parents *were* married. There is no doubt about it! Do you imagine that my family would have allowed me to associate with you if they weren't? Heaven forbid!"

"But Belle—"

"I shall not tell you what I think of Belle. Besides, somebody in your family must know where your parents were married. Why not ask Arthur? Or Fernand?"

Lucinda sighed forlornly. "They are not here. And I cannot go to them."

"Why not?"

"If I go after Arthur, Fernand will come back, find nobody here and go haring off. If I go after Fernand, Arthur will come back, find nobody here and—"

"Oh. I see." Zoë grimaced. "Where is Fernand?"

Lucinda shrugged. "On his way to Gretna Green, I think. I'm not sure."

"Hmm. Well, in that case I shall contact Arthur for you."

"Arthur? You?"

"Yes. I should love it. I know exactly where to find him. And meanwhile, if Fernand returns..."

"I know. Hang on to him!" It was easier said than done, she knew. "But, Zoë, are you sure?"

"Yes, indeed. It will give me something to do while Vincent is down in Plymouth."

"Plymouth?"

"Didn't I say? Yes, Plymouth."

"But you went to London to see his family, and..."

Zoë nodded vigorously. "We went to London *first*, not just to see our families, but also to see my godmother, Lady Zoë Grixby. It so happened that we mentioned Belle to her, saying she was born in Saint James's Palace. Lady Zoë immediately answered that she wasn't, not in all the time she had been there."

"Goodness!"

"Vincent and I of course defended Belle, but Lady Zoë was adamant. It was not just that she did not recollect Belle having been born there. She insisted it simply was not possible."

"Oh, dear!"

"Naturally, Vincent was determined to convince Lady Zoë, for Belle's sake...."

"Naturally."

"...so he went to the Admiralty to see if anyone remembered Admiral Anstruther and could vouch for Belle's having been born in Saint James's Palace."

"And?"

Zoë lowered her voice and whispered, "It seems that Belle has not been entirely honest with us. Vincent has gone to Plymouth to verify the details, but depend upon it, the story Belle spun for us is worthy of a three-volume novel for its inventiveness and colourful characterizations!"

"COME IN!" snapped the Earl of Sarne.

The door opened.

Lord Sarne did not turn round. His gaze was fixed upon the woods in the distance. So angry was he, that if his temper had been a match, he would have used it to burn them down.

Mr. Liggatt stepped into the study and closed the door with a click behind him.

"Well?" demanded Lord Sarne, still without bothering to turn.

"Miss Fitzjames and Miss Anstruther are in the west drawing room, my lord."

Lord Sarne faced him. His expression was cold and forbidding.

Mr. Liggatt knew in an instant why none of the servants had wished to enter.

"What the devil are you telling me this for?" snarled the earl.

Mr. Liggatt stood his ground. "Miss Anstruther and Miss Fitzjames particularly requested that you should be so informed."

Lord Sarne's jet-black eyes glinted with anger. An acid curse sprang to his lips.

He did not need Mr. Liggatt to tell him that even now Bellemaine was stretched out upon the chaise longue, or that Nona Fitzjames was sitting on the window seat, admiring, for the millionth time, the west drawing room's dark oak panelling with its heavy Jacobean carving.

No gift of prophesy was necessary. It was easy to deduce the purpose of the message. Lord Sarne was expected to rush to the west drawing room, fall upon his knees and request Bellemaine's hand in marriage. Nona Fitzjames would be the unimpeachable witness of their betrothal.

Lord Sarne ground his teeth. He surmised that it was not Nona who lay behind the scheme, but Bellemaine. *Does she expect me to jump whenever she snaps her fingers?* he wondered bitterly.

"How long have they been there?" he rasped.

"In the drawing room, my lord?" asked Mr. Liggatt.

"No, damn you! In the house!"

Mr. Liggatt stiffened. It was ten years since he had been addressed in that tone. "Ten days, my lord."

Lord Sarne sensed the pain he had given the other man. Briefly, he shut his eyes. "I'm sorry, Liggatt."

Mr. Liggatt inclined his head in acknowledgement of the apology.

"Serve them lunch. Keep them occupied. Tell them I'm busy. That I can't be disturbed. Anything you like!" added the earl.

"Very good, my lord." Mr. Liggatt stepped out of the room. Realph, the butler, was waiting. "His lordship," said Mr. Liggatt quietly, "does not wish to be disturbed."

Realph pursed his lips. "The ladies were most insistent."

Mr. Liggatt shrugged.

"This is the third time..." ventured Realph.

Mr. Liggatt was frowning worriedly. "They must be kept away from him."

Realph's eyebrows rose in query.

"His lordship has something on his mind," explained Mr. Liggatt.

"Hmm. Very good, Mr. Liggatt." The butler clicked his heels and departed. "I shall see to it."

Mr. Liggatt, still wearing the frown which had been with him since he had seen Lord Sarne, entered the kitchen. There was only one person in it at that hour, it being Sunday.

"Good morning, Mrs. Pott."

The aptly named head cook responded with her customary country drawl and usage. "They say his lordship be in a black humour this morning."

"He has something on his mind."

Mrs. Pott was elbow-deep in strong dough—a favourite pastime of hers. "Has he then?"

Mr. Liggatt prowled around her until, with her eyes, she indicated a plateful of assorted tarts, from which he helped himself. "It's not like him." He took a bite. "Excellent tarts, Mrs. Pott."

Mrs. Pott grinned. "Thank'ee." She pummelled the dough. "They say Miss Anstruther and Miss Fitzjames be here still."

Mr. Liggatt, his mouth full, nodded.

"They say Miss Anstruther be wanting a proposal from his lordship."

"She can want that until she is blue in the face."

"Oh, yes?"

"It's my opinion Lord Sarne looks elsewhere."

"Ah! You wouldn't be after telling me who?"

Mr. Liggatt whispered in her ear. "Miss Lucinda Edrington."

"Ah! She be a good choice for him. I'd like her as a mistress. I hear good things of her." Mrs. Pott paused and reflected. "Something on his lordship's mind, you say? Happen she said no to him?"

Mr. Liggatt shrugged.

"She'd be a fool if she did," judged Mrs. Pott. "Unless . . . you don't suppose there is something wrong?"

"Hmm," mumbled Mr. Liggatt.

Mrs. Pott contemplated him shrewdly. "Speaking of marriage, you be not married yourself, Mr. Liggatt."

"I've thought about it." He had swallowed his tart. "But I haven't found the right woman yet."

"Ah. You've not met Hebe Ursell then?"

"No."

"A man like you could do a lot worse than Hebe Ursell over at Bluebell Manor."

Mr. Liggatt pricked up his ears. "In service, is she?"

Mrs. Pott nodded. "To Miss Lucinda Edrington."

A glance was exchanged.

"Mrs. Pott, I am obliged to you."

LUCK WAS WITH MR. LIGGATT. He found Lucinda's maid in the garden collecting flowers for a posy.

Hebe Ursell was surprised—and not a little alarmed—that such a fine wealthy man as himself should come calling upon her. But when she learned, in confidence, that he had only acted as Lord Sarne's agent at the auction, her mind was considerably eased.

For his part, Mr. Liggatt found Hebe easy to converse with. She was, as Mrs. Pott had hinted, attractive and practical. She could keep her own counsel. He need not fear that anything he said would go any further.

He was much taken with her, and felt that she was everything he could want in a wife.

She seemed much taken with him also, and it was not long before he was telling her about the Earl of Sarne, and how worried he was about him.

"...and when he came back from church this morning, he was in a foul temper. It may be that he proposed to Miss Edrington and she refused him."

"I wouldn't be knowing about that," replied Hebe, with the same drawl and usage as Mrs. Pott.

"He did meet her. I know it for a fact." Mr. Liggatt paused. "She wouldn't play with a man, would she?"

"If you knew Miss Edrington, you wouldn't even think that!"

"The trouble is, I don't know her. I couldn't begin to guess what might have gone wrong."

"You asking me to tell you her secrets?" Hebe's eyes glinted with sudden anger.

"Forgive me. I wouldn't normally." Mr. Liggatt frowned. "I've known Lord Sarne for many years. It's through him I had my education. We were at Oxford together. I served under him in the Peninsula. I would lay down my life for him, and there are not many men I would say that about."

Hebe twisted her apron. "I been in service here with Miss Edrington since I were thirteen years old. My mother were in service with her mother, and my grandmother with her grandmother. Now you come here—a stranger—asking me to tell you private things what have happened in the family. Well, I won't!"

"She's in trouble, isn't she?"

Hebe went on cutting flowers.

"Lord Sarne could probably help her."

"If she thinks he can, I'm sure she'll ask him."

Mr. Liggatt shuffled his feet. "I've seen Lord Sarne like this once before—and only once. It was the bloodiest, most awful event of both our lives."

CHAPTER SIXTEEN

"Do you remember," Mr. Liggatt asked Hebe solemnly, "when Sir John Moore's army was on the retreat to Corunna?"

"I've heard of it," Hebe replied.

"It was winter. Boney beat us back. There was nothing to do but retreat. We were in northern Spain, in the hills. It was bitterly cold. We had no food, no wood for fires. We had no drink. Our clothes were wet. Our boots were frozen. We marched in sleet and hail. We bivouacked in the snow."

"I have heard that terrible things happened on that retreat."

Mr. Liggatt nodded. "Black Bob Craufurd pulled the rearguard together. He whipped us into order again." He drew a deep breath. "We made it through the hills down to the warm, sunny plains. Then we saw food. Unripe fruit. Green corn. The worst kind of food. We were so hungry—" He broke off abruptly. "Some ate it. Some died and some went mad."

Hebe's eyes were on his hands. They were fine, long-fingered hands, like a gentleman's, but tightly clenched. His knuckles were white.

"Lord Sarne was a lot younger then." Mr. Liggatt paused. "I thought he would crack. He had been used to high living, you see, and fine things. He did something I'd never seen an officer do before. He got off his horse and he walked. He made us keep pace. He drove us hard. He wouldn't let us rest—if we had, we would have frozen where we sat. But he walked alongside us. He didn't ride. He wouldn't let us touch that bad food. Some men cursed him for it, but when others lay dying, we—''

"You knew he had been right," Hebe supplied.

"Yes. We fought a battle at Corunna."

"Sir John Moore was killed then, they say."

"Yes. But thanks to his stand, we were able to embark on our ships. If we hadn't fought off the French there, the British Army would never have been evacuated. We would have rotted in French prisons."

He gave a short, humourless laugh as a memory came back to him. "The Spanish generals, the old ones, used us like dogs. But the Spanish people at Corunna risked everything to help us. They gave their word that they would support us if the French attacked. We knew they would keep their word." He was trembling. "They crossed themselves when they saw us leave. We were a bunch of dirty scarecrows with bleeding feet and filthy faces."

Hebe's eyes were wide.

"Lord Sarne carried me on to our ship. He looked back at Corunna where they buried Sir John Moore. It was then I saw that look: haunted, bitter, filled with the fires of hell. I saw it again on his face today...."

There was a long silence.

Suddenly, Hebe began cutting the flowers with unaccustomed vigour. "Well, I'll tell you, but it must go no further—not anyone but his lordship, mind!"

"You have my word."

Hebe dipped her head. "I have heard," she murmured softly, "that Miss Edrington cannot find the record of her parents' marriage. I have heard that Miss Bellemaine Anstruther says there be not one."

Mr. Liggatt's jaw sagged. "You mean she is illegitimate?"

"Lord love you, no! Not if you're asking me! Three generations of my family have served three generations of hers. There be no by-blows in that house. Her parents were married right enough!"

"Well then . . ."

"Miss Bellemaine Anstruther be after something. That's my guess. Or someone. If you take my meaning."

LORD SARNE HAD PUT ON his high military boots and his finest buckskin breeches. He wore a royal-blue riding coat. His white lawn cravat was as stiff and formal as his manner and a monocle adorned his right eye.

"I have decided to close Sarne Abbey. It displeases me," he announced. "We shall return to London at once. Please give the necessary orders."

"Very good, my lord." If Mr. Liggatt was surprised, he gave no sign of it.

Lord Sarne waited for his protest, with several scathing retorts at the ready. When no objection came, he turned away from Mr. Liggatt and toward the study window once more. He touched the diamond panes lightly, caressing them as if they were precious jewels.

Mr. Liggatt cleared his throat.

Lord Sarne glanced at him. "What is it?"

"I have been to Bluebell Manor, my lord."

"I know. The entire household knows. By tomorrow the whole county will be aware of it. At least two hundred people have seen fit to inform me that you went to pay court to Hebe Ursell, who is a maid there."

Mr. Liggatt's lips twitched. "One can only marvel at how swiftly news spreads in the country, my lord. If we had had such communications in Spain, we would have beaten Boney in half the time."

Unexpectedly, Lord Sarne smiled. His aquiline features were illuminated. "Yes, we would have, wouldn't we?"

"Did anyone happen to mention the, um, other purpose of my visit?"

Lord Sarne frowned and shook his head.

"It is as well," remarked Mr. Liggatt, "for it concerned Miss Edrington. And Miss Ursell would be even more distressed than I if she thought it had become common knowledge."

Mr. Liggatt knew he had Lord Sarne's attention now. The earl had neither spoken nor moved since he had mentioned Lucinda's name. His very stillness invited Mr. Liggatt to proceed.

"It seems," said Mr. Liggatt, "that Miss Edrington cannot find the record of her parents' marriage. It is not in Saint Peter's Church. Nor in the chapel here at the Abbey. Miss Anstruther has hinted that there was no marriage."

Lord Sarne's black eyebrows lifted. His monocle dropped from his eye and hung forgotten on its ribbon. "And Miss Ursell believes this?"

"Oh, no, my lord. Miss Ursell is devoted to her mistress. She is convinced a record of the marriage exists."

Lord Sarne left the window. He paced up and down between the glass-fronted bookshelves and the rose-wood writing desk. "Belay my first orders, Liggatt. We're staying here after all. Have my horse saddled and at the front door as soon as possible."

"It is already waiting, my lord."

Lord Sarne's quick smile appeared again. He gripped Mr. Liggatt's shoulders in a gesture of affection. Then he shot out of the room.

HEBE EXPECTED Lord Sarne's arrival. She had induced the other servants to say nothing, for Miss Edrington's sake.

Thus, when the earl reached Bluebell Manor, his horse was put out of sight and he was directed discreetly to the maze. He did not walk into it. He ran.

ZOË HAD GONE to find Arthur.

"He has a head like a sieve when it comes to family history," Lucinda had warned. "But I daresay you will get something out of him."

"I will, my dear!" Zoë had promised. "Depend upon it. Melissa will help me. If Arthur has any memory of where your parents were married, we shall drag it out of him.''

"Poor Arthur! I almost pity him his fate!''

Zoë had departed with a laugh and an exhortation not to worry.

Not worry? Lucinda thought bitterly as she retied the ribbons on her hat. *How can I not worry?*

Slowly, she wandered into the maze. She was so preoccupied with her problems that she did not hear footsteps crunching on the gravel. She was aware of nothing until she was swept into a crushing embrace, and Lord Sarne's voice sounded in her ear, saying, "Never do that again!''

Lucinda did not speak. Her coral lips, her blushing cheeks, her slender white hands were being covered with kisses. The poignancy of the moment was too sweet, too exquisite for words.

"Promise me!'' The Earl of Sarne's voice was a hoarse whisper. "Promise me that if ever you have a problem—any problem—you'll tell me. Promise me!''

"I . . . I promise.'' Lucinda's answer was as faint as the leaves rustling in the summer breeze.

"Lucinda!'' he breathed passionately. "Lucinda!''

His arms still encircled her. Her body was pressed against his. She could feel the blood pounding through his veins.

"H-how did you find . . .'' she began.

"Luck. One of my people discovered you had been looking for a record of your parents' marriage.''

The light went out of Lucinda's brown eyes. Her mouth curved down. "You know, then, that I couldn't find it.''

He nodded.

"You see now why I can't accept—"

She was pushing him away. His hands tightened abruptly.

"You are *not* illegitimate!" he said firmly. "And even if you were, do you think I'd give a damn?"

Lucinda's delicate features clouded. "But you ought to. You're the Earl of Sarne and you—"

His fingers brushed against her lips, silencing her. He made her sit down on a bench beside him. "I love you, Lucinda."

Unable to meet his burning gaze, she bowed her head. Her cheeks were as pink as the ribbons on her hat.

"I love you," he went on, "not the entry of your parents' marriage in a dusty old register."

Lucinda giggled. "Well, that is one way of looking at it."

He almost smiled. "Now, tell me you will marry me."

She gazed at him in alarm. "But I cannot. Not until—"

He stopped her with more kisses, fiery kisses that left her breathless with joy.

"Do not dare to tell me you *cannot* marry me! Tell me you *won't* marry me. Tell me you love another. But do not tell me you *cannot* marry me!"

"But . . ."

The proof—the proof of her parents' marriage— was all-important. With it, she could hold her head up high in society. Without it, she was disgraced. Could he not see that?

"No buts. I must know that you are mine!"

His tone made Lucinda glance up sharply. His black eyes held an expression she had never seen before in anyone's—man's or woman's. He yearned for her. And his yearning was tinged with fear. A strange wonderment spread through her.

He is afraid of losing me!

She realized that his hand was trembling very slightly as he held hers. She saw that he had placed a ring upon her finger. A sapphire, tied with a golden lovers' knot.

Her reason disapproved. It spoke of propriety and convention. It mentioned the need for her parents' union to have been solemnized—in church. It warned of the serious consequences had such a solemnization not taken place.

Her heart told her the things that truly mattered: *You love him. You couldn't marry anyone else. He loves you. He wants you even if the whole of England calls you a bastard. Why do you hesitate?*

CHAPTER SEVENTEEN

LUCINDA'S HEART WON. "Yes. I will marry you. I love you, Gabriel . . . very much."

The Earl of Sarne swept her into his arms once more. Their lips met, and time was suspended. . . .

The noisy clearing of Hebe's throat made Lord Sarne and Lucinda break apart. The maid stood before them, wringing her apron in her hands and hopping from one foot to the other.

"I'm sorry to interrupt, Miss Edrington, your lordship."

Lucinda raised her hand instinctively to her hair. Her bonnet had come off, and so had her mobcap. Lord Sarne had been running his fingers through her curls. She was certain they were a sight.

"What is it, Hebe?"

"Well, everyone be here and we've run out of rooms to put them in, see. We done our best, but there be no more rooms. So we don't know what to do with them."

"Everyone? What do you mean by everyone?"

Hebe took a deep breath. "Well, Mr. and Mrs. Bushens and the Marquis de Niverne turned up together. . . ."

"Oh dear!" interpolated Lucinda.

". . . so we put them in the drawing room," continued Hebe. "Then Mr. Edrington and Miss-Bushens-that-was—but now she's Mrs. Edrington—and Miss Joliffe came. We put them in the library. Then we had Miss Fitzjames and Miss Anstruther. We put them in the music room. And then—"

"You mean there are more?" demanded Lord Sarne.

"Oh, yes, your lordship," Hebe assured him solemnly. "Begging your pardon, but someone—Miss Anstruther, we think—let Sir Kirby Hookmeadow in. He's hiding in the dining room, hoping to see you, Miss Edrington."

Lord Sarne's face darkened with anger. He bit back a furious oath.

"And then," said Hebe, "we had—"

"Not another!" gasped Lucinda.

"And then we had," continued Hebe stolidly, "the Marchioness of Niverne. She be in the morning room, where she can lie down, quiet-like. And then we had Mr. Liggatt and Lord Overberry come together, wanting to know where you be, my lord. We thought of putting them in the breakfast room. But the carpenters be working there, so we put them on the terrace, because we didn't have anywhere else to put them."

Lucinda and Lord Sarne exchanged glances. Unconsciously, their fingers touched, then their hands curled round each other.

"You have done very well," Lucinda complimented her maid.

"Yes, you have," agreed Lord Sarne.

"Thank'ee." Hebe blushed and curtseyed to them both.

Lord Sarne was thoughtful. "Let us deal with them one at a time. Could you ask Lord Overberry and Mr. Liggatt to come here, please?"

"Yes, my lord." Hebe dropped another curtsey before she hurried out of the maze.

"CONGRATULATE US!" announced Lord Sarne. "We are engaged to be married!"

"Congratulations!" Lord Overberry kissed Lucinda and embraced his friend.

Mr. Liggatt smiled and bowed. "Congratulations, Miss Edrington. Congratulations, my lord. May I wish you every happiness?"

"Thank you," murmured Lucinda.

"Many thanks," returned Lord Sarne. "Now, what brings you both here?"

"I have been investigating Bellemaine Anstruther," said Lord Overberry.

"Oh?" quipped Lord Sarne. "Did you discover any juicy scandals?"

Lord Overberry grinned. "I certainly did! I came to Sarne Abbey to tell you. On the way I met Liggatt." He indicated his companion. "*He* was coming here to inform you that Belle and Nona Fitzjames had left there and—"

"I know," said Lord Sarne wryly. "They are here."

Mr. Liggatt nodded.

"So, I came with him instead," continued Lord Overberry. "Would you like to know what I discovered concerning Belle?"

"Of course, but—" Lord Sarne paused, considering "—we have such a collection of guests in the house! They all want seeing to and we must arrange things properly—" Again he stopped and then asked mischievously, "By the way, you wouldn't happen to have unearthed anything regarding Sir Kirby Hookmeadow?"

"Yes, indeed." Lord Overberry's eyes twinkled. "He won't be pleased when I tax him with it, either."

"Excellent!" Lord Sarne did not bother to hide his delight. "I'll be with you in a moment."

As Mr. Liggatt and Lord Overberry disappeared from view, Lord Sarne turned back to Lucinda. His face was no longer smiling.

Lucinda realized she was expected to make some comment. "I thought Mr. Liggatt was a wealthy gentleman, yet he deferred to you as if..."

Lord Sarne was tense, as if afraid of her reaction. "He was my agent at the auction. He bought Bluebell Manor for me."

Her eyes widened. Her lips parted. "You paid far more...than it was worth."

He smiled and lifted his shoulders in a slight shrug. "It depends on how one values...the place."

His eyes were caressing her. A warm glow of happiness spread through her. So he had not deserted her at the auction—he had been thinking of her all the while. Suddenly her forehead wrinkled.

"Did Zoë know?"

"Not at first. She made bids on her own account. Then I asked her to bid for me until Liggatt arrived. She promised to say nothing to anyone."

"She has not breathed a word," returned Lucinda.

"I would have been more open, but I suspected Sir Kirby was up to something. The message did not sound quite genuine to me, yet I could not afford to ignore it." He paused briefly. "I never suspected Belle!"

"Neither did I," murmured Lucinda. "Not until . . . much later."

"Yes." For a moment his expression was bitter. Then his face cleared and he smiled at her. "Do you want to go on living at Bluebell Manor?"

Lucinda considered. "It means more to Arthur. He loves the farm."

Lord Sarne nodded. "I felt it might. We talked it over, he and I. He suggested, if you don't mind, that he and Melissa should live here. Then he could go on farming. He is good at it. It shouldn't be long before he turns a profit. . . ."

". . . and then he'll insist on repaying you."

Lord Sarne held himself in check. "We'll worry about that when it happens." His black eyes met her brown ones. "You are content to be mistress of Sarne Abbey?"

Lucinda reflected. "It's bigger than Bluebell Manor, and I shall have to get used to it, but yes, I could be . . . happy there."

Her answer won a kiss from him. It was some time before he went on, "We shall make it a happy place, a home for our children." He gestured expressively. "Oh, and before I forget, Arthur wants to cut down the stables—he feels you were both keeping too many horses."

"Yes." They had far too many horses. And yet...what would become of Pearl?

"I bought one of them for you—Pearl. She—" Suddenly he stopped.

Tears were trickling down Lucinda's cheeks.

The earl drew a deep, shuddering breath. His fingers brushed her tears away.

"Why are you crying?"

Her voice was so soft he could scarcely hear it. "You are so...good to me."

He held her close and kissed away her tears.

When Lucinda had fully regained her composure, she went into the drawing room. Fernand was seated on the sofa. A great oak walking stick was beside him. His left leg was heavily bandaged and rested on a footstool.

Mr. and Mrs. Bushens, frigid and disapproving, were seated on the very edges of a pair of chairs alongside him.

"Fernand!" gasped Lucinda. "What happened to your leg?"

"It's nothing." Fernand wore a brave expression. "A sprain, no more." He made as if to rise and winced with pain.

"No, don't get up," pleaded Lucinda. "Mrs. Bushens, Mr. Bushens—" She started to welcome them to the house.

Mrs. Bushens cut her short. "We have been waiting a good thirty minutes!"

"I am very sorry."

"So you should be! And as for sending us on that wild-goose chase—"

"I did not send you on any wild-goose chase!"

"No? Did you not mention Gretna Green? Did you not say your brother here—" she gestured angrily at Fernand "—thought that Melissa and Arthur had gone to Gretna Green?"

"I did. But you rushed off before I could finish. If you had waited—"

"Waited? What!" interrupted Mr. Bushens. "We were consumed with anxiety for Melissa! How could we possibly wait?"

"Melissa is quite safe," Lucinda assured them.

"Safe, is she?" challenged Mrs. Bushens. "And what about her reputation? Ruined! Past recall! Thanks to you and your infernal brothers!"

"Mrs. Bushens, you can hardly blame Fernand," retorted Lucinda. "He did his very best to find Melissa and to restore her to you."

"His very best? Then I shudder to think what his very worst can be! I found him nursing a sprained ankle which had swollen up to the size of a melon and all he can say is that he has had time to reflect, and on second thoughts he feels his brother would definitely *not* have taken Melissa to Gretna Green!"

"How did you sprain it, Fernand?" enquired Lucinda, hoping to change the subject.

Fernand blushed. "I, er, slipped . . . on the staircase at the inn. I was . . . walking too fast."

"Harrumph!" Mr. Bushens snorted contemptuously. "Typically French! Never look where they are going. If Bonaparte had looked before he leapt, he would never have ended up on Saint Helena."

Fernand ground his teeth.

"So we returned here with the invalid," continued Mrs. Bushens, "and what happened? We were kept waiting for thirty minutes! What is the meaning of this?"

"Yes, what is the meaning of this?" echoed Mr. Bushens.

"It was not intentional," soothed Lucinda. She might as well have tried to placate two angry thunderclouds.

"I'm glad to hear it!" exclaimed Mrs. Bushens frostily.

"What I would like to know is, what has become of our daughter?" insisted Mr. Bushens. "And when may we take her home?"

"I think there is something you should know," said Lucinda. "Melissa and Arthur were married by special licence, which she bought, in Canterbury. The Archbishop officiated."

There was a sharp intake of breath.

"Lord Sarne witnessed the wedding," resumed Lucinda. "So did Lord Overberry and his fiancée, Zoë Joliffe. Knowing Zoë, I shouldn't be surprised if she had Melissa and Arthur presented to the Prince Regent the very next day. She is very good at arranging Court presentations."

Mrs. Bushens's jaw sagged. As Lucinda finished her speech, she slid off her chair and fell insensible to the floor.

Mr. Bushens looked down at her.

Fernand looked down at her.

Lucinda looked down at her. "Oh dear. I'll get some smelling salts." She ran to the door, then stopped. "Fernand, you wouldn't by any chance happen to know where Mama and Papa were married, would you?"

Fernand blinked at her. "I? Of course not. Why should I? I was less than a year old at the time!"

"You might have asked them later."

"I didn't."

"You should have. It was most inconsiderate of you not to!"

Fernand gazed at her in astonishment. By the time he had a suitable reply ready, she had left the room.

NONA FITZJAMES was seated at the pianoforte, playing a delightful sonata by Mozart. She was an accomplished pianist and the sonata sounded well.

Lord Sarne would have let her finish the piece but she became aware of his entrance and stopped playing at once. "Gabriel! At last! Belle and I have been trying to see you all morning! Your servants kept telling us that you were busy! And then, just by chance, we learned that you had come here, so..."

"I was busy, Cousin Nona!" Lord Sarne bowed, acknowledging both ladies as he strode to the centre of the room. "Belle! How nice to see you again! Do forgive me for not seeing you at Sarne Abbey, but I have been...extremely busy." He smiled broadly at both of them. "I have become engaged...to Lucinda Edrington."

Nona Fitzjames's eyes widened and her eyebrows rose to a dizzy height. She glanced from Lord Sarne to Bellemaine. In a trice, her position was decided.

"Allow me to offer my felicitations, Gabriel. I hope you and Lucinda will be very happy."

"Thank you, Cousin Nona," replied the earl.

"And now, if you will excuse me—" Nona was on her feet. "—I must find Lucinda and wish her every happiness, too. Are you coming with me, Belle?"

"I shall join you later." Bellemaine's eyes glinted with rage, and she struggled to keep her smile in place. As the door closed behind Nona Fitzjames, she turned to Lord Sarne. "This is very sudden, Gabriel."

Lord Sarne seated himself. Absently, he ran his hand through his black hair. "It is far from sudden, Belle."

"But you have not known Lucinda very long."

"Long enough to decide that she should be my countess."

Bellemaine flicked her fan open and shut. "I would congratulate you, but I very much fear that my congratulations may be, er, misplaced."

"Why so?"

Bellemaine sighed. She gazed at those fine hands for whose beauty she was famed. "You have not by any chance investigated Lucinda's . . . antecedents?"

Lord Sarne was silent.

"I have heard rumours," continued Bellemaine, "that Lucinda's parents were, ahem, not married."

An angry flush darkened Lord Sarne's face. With an effort, he made himself smile. "I do hope that you have not been *spreading* these rumours."

"Of course not, Gabriel!" Bellemaine was all innocence.

"I am glad to hear it."

Bellemaine inclined her head. "There have also been rumours that Lucinda is to marry—" she coughed "—Sir Kirby Hookmeadow, with whom, they say, she is passionately in love."

Lord Sarne's hands clenched. He made no comment.

Bellemaine cast a sidelong glance in his direction. "The trouble is that, if these rumours are true..."

"They are not." The denial was swift and sharp.

"But if they are," murmured Bellemaine, "if Lucinda is, er, illegitimate...she would be *safer* married to Sir Kirby."

"Safer?" Lord Sarne's voice was dangerously quiet.

"As Countess of Sarne, she would be in the public eye. Her private life would come under intense scrutiny. The merest whisper of scandal would bring out all the worst in people."

Lord Sarne froze.

"As Sir Kirby Hookmeadow's wife, however, she would not be subject to such...scrutiny."

"Rumours do not die simply because one changes one's marriage partner!"

Bellemaine smiled. "But you forget, Gabriel, Sir Kirby is well known in the county. Any rumour about his wife would be instantly discounted. His reputation would protect her."

A muscle in Lord Sarne's cheek throbbed. "You are being offensive."

"I?" Bellemaine's hand flew to her breast. "Forgive me, Gabriel. That was hardly my intention."

His expression did not soften.

"Do you not see? If Lucinda were Sir Kirby Hook-meadow's wife, the rumours would die. But if she becomes Countess of Sarne, there will be no chance of quashing them. It breaks my heart to have to tell you this, Gabriel, but your long absence has made people, er, rather inquisitive about you. You have already set every tongue in Dorset wagging."

"I don't follow you."

"People will naturally be curious about the woman you marry, and if it is to be Lucinda..."

"Yes?"

"...interest in her would be awakened. Every titbit, every item of gossip would be discussed—one might say chewed to pieces. The story about her parents not having been married would be too good to miss. You know how people are." Her eyes melted with sympathy. "Lucinda is already upset. Such unrelenting persecution! Why, I am afraid it would kill her!"

CHAPTER EIGHTEEN

"SO YOU BELIEVE I should give Lucinda up?" enquired Lord Sarne silkily.

Bellemaine's shoulders lifted the merest fraction. "I am so concerned for you both. This matter of the missing proof of Lucinda's parents' marriage cannot be concealed. People will be bound to investigate. They will find out. They..."

"They will never find out, because the rumours are unfounded."

Bellemaine pouted. "If you say so."

"I *do* say so."

In a trice, Bellemaine saw she had lost. Grimacing, she stood up.

Immediately, Lord Sarne leapt to his feet.

"In that case," Bellemaine said as she retied her bonnet, "I do most sincerely offer you my congratulations, Gabriel. I hope we shall always be friends. And if there is anything I can ever do to help you, please do not hesitate to call upon me."

Lord Sarne raised Bellemaine's fingers to his lips. There was a hint of menace in his tone. "I shall not forget this, Belle."

LUCINDA DASHED into the library.

"Lucinda!" Zoë, Melissa and Arthur cried at once.

"Where have you been? We've been waiting for ages!"

Lucinda launched forth. "Melissa, your parents are in the drawing room. Your mother has fainted."

Melissa shot out of the library to the rescue.

"Arthur, Fernand has arrived with the Bushens. He has sprained his ankle. He is in the drawing room, too."

Arthur vanished in the same direction as his wife.

"Zoë, did Arthur remember where our parents were married?"

Zoë shook her head. "He says that they never told him, that he never asked."

Lucinda clicked her tongue. "How inconsiderate of him!"

"Doesn't Fernand know?"

"No. His answer was the same as Arthur's."

"But your parents must have told *someone*! After all, it is not as if it is a shameful secret."

"If they *were* married."

"Of course they were married. I keep telling you so." Zoë sighed deeply. "Let's rejoin the others, and see if we can dig it out of one of them!"

"OH!" GASPED NONA FITZJAMES. "You frightened me, Vincent!"

Lord Overberry bowed. "I beg your pardon."

"Granted. What are you doing here?"

"I was looking for Zoë."

"Is she here?"

"Yes, somewhere."

"Indeed? I have not seen her."

"One of the servants told me she was somewhere about. Perhaps Gabriel knows. Have you seen him?"

"Yes. He is in the music room, talking with Belle." Nona Fitzjames rummaged in her butterscotch-velvet reticule for her smelling salts. "He gave me quite a shock, you know. Told me he is engaged to Lucinda Edrington."

Lord Overberry studied her. "Yes, you do look a bit white. Perhaps you should sit down."

The door to the library was open. There was no one inside. Lord Overberry led Nona Fitzjames there, placed her in the most comfortable armchair and stood solicitously over her. Nona Fitzjames, breathing heavily, applied the smelling salts with vigour. "What do you think of that, eh? What do you think of Gabriel becoming engaged to Lucinda?"

"I think Gabriel will be very happy with Lucinda. As happy as I am going to be with Zoë."

"Hah! Melissa's a fool, you know. *You* would have been better for her than Arthur. Still, I wish you joy. Zoë Joliffe is presentable—and well connected."

"Er, thank you."

Nona Fitzjames snorted like a horse. "As for Gabriel and Lucinda, I wish I shared your confidence. Lucinda is . . . is . . . ." She gesticulated helplessly.

"So you thought Gabriel ought to marry Belle?"

"She seemed an excellent choice."

"*Seemed*, Nona."

Nona Fitzjames fastened him with a beady eye. "What do you know that I do not?"

"I have been investigating Belle's background." Lord Overberry seated himself opposite the lady, and stretched his legs out in front of him. "I was worried, you see. A chance remark by Zoë's godmother was what—started me. She cast doubt upon Belle, and—" he sighed deeply "—I wanted to defend her. I ended by exposing her."

"Explain."

"There was no Admiral Anstruther."

Nona Fitzjames frowned. "But the stories she told—they were so very like the fifth earl!"

"Oh the *stories* were genuine, but Belle's father was not an Admiral. He was an ordinary able-bodied seaman."

Nona Fitzjames drew her lips together in grim disapproval. "I see."

"He served under Gabriel's grandfather, so one might say he *did* know him...."

"Harrumph!" Nona Fitzjames's pupils narrowed to pinpoints. "So! And Belle was not born at Saint James's Palace, either, I presume?"

"Not at *the* Saint James's Palace, you mean."

"Explain."

"She was born in Plymouth, in a house known mockingly as Saint James's Palace."

Nona Fitzjames was sitting bolt upright. The smelling salts had disappeared. A spot of anger burned in each cheek. "And where did Belle acquire her fortune? Or is that, too, a mere fiction?"

Lord Overberry stared at his riding boots. "Belle's father and mother engaged in certain ventures of, er, a questionable nature. They made a great deal of money. Belle inherited it. She has a way with money. She invested wisely..."

"Well!" Colour suffused Nona Fitzjames's face. "Good gracious me! How I have been deceived! To think that I actually considered Belle a fit wife for Gabriel. What must he think of me?"

"I am sure Gabriel will forgive you."

"I shall never forgive myself."

"You couldn't possibly have known."

"I am mortified!"

"You need not be. Belle was very clever. She took us all in. Discovering the truth about her was extremely difficult."

Nona Fitzjames placed her withered, bony hand on his firm, strong one. "You are too kind, Vincent." She smiled bravely. "Does Gabriel know?"

Lord Overberry nodded. "I told Gabriel—and Lucinda—a few minutes ago, before we came into the house."

"But you and Gabriel did not come in together, did you?"

"No. Gabriel asked me to see to something first." He paused. "They also know about Sir Kirby Hookmeadow."

Nona Fitzjames eyed Lord Overberry curiously. "What about Sir Kirby Hookmeadow?"

"Not only is he mortgaged to the hilt, through heavy borrowing, but I have discovered that he has offered his property as security for its entire value to two different banks!"

Nona Fitzjames pursed her lips. "That was very foolish of him. But can he not repay the money?"

Lord Overberry shook his head. "He has spent a large part of it. He had expectations, you see, of acquiring Bluebell Manor."

"I don't understand."

Lord Overberry brushed a piece of fluff from his brown sleeve. "Sir Kirby Hookmeadow was determined to have the estate. He had information about Bluebell Manor, or at least Lucinda's half of it, which made him believe that it was worth a fortune."

"What information?"

"Sir Kirby heard a legend that there is a diamond mine on the property."

Nona Fitzjames clapped her hands. "Good heavens!"

"Gabriel thought it was nonsense when I told him. So did Arthur. But Sir Kirby was convinced that no legend is entirely without foundation. He went into the matter. He discovered a map of Lucinda's half of the property on which the diamond mine was marked."

Nona Fitzjames's eyebrows were raised.

"That, to him, was proof enough of its existence," continued Lord Overberry. "He started to buy mining equipment—"

"Well!"

"As far as Sir Kirby was able to ascertain, without giving himself away, neither Arthur nor Lucinda knew anything about the mine. It seemed to have been unexplored and its existence, although known for more than a hundred years, appeared to have been forgotten. Sir Kirby thought, therefore, that it would be an easy matter to persuade Arthur and Lucinda to sell."

"Tsk! Tsk!"

"Sir Kirby was excited about the possibilities of the mine. He guessed that it would be worth millions. Untold millions. He had to have it."

"What did Lucinda say to this, or haven't you told her?"

"I told her. She thought the same as Gabriel and Arthur. She said her parents had told her that there was a story about a diamond mine, but that it was not true."

Nona Fitzjames coughed delicately. "She has more sense than I gave her credit for."

"I beg your pardon?"

"But that Sir Kirby could be taken in. That he has actually fallen for that old wives' tale. I am astounded! Truly astounded!"

"Fallen for?" Lord Overberry was startled. "Old wives' tale?"

Nona Fitzjames was smiling. "That's right. It's nothing more than an old wives' tale."

"But the evidence. The map. The legend. The source of the story!"

"Bah! The source of the story, indeed! I'll tell you the source of the story!"

"Please do."

"Something over a hundred years ago, a cave was discovered on what is now Lucinda's half of Bluebell Manor. It was a damp, cold cave, with strange formations like melting candles lining the floor and the roof. Water dripped from them and when a lantern was shone into the dampness, the area sparkled like so many diamonds. One of the Edringtons wrote a pretty sonnet, referring to 'the diamonds underground.'"

"And from this the legend grew?"

"Precisely."

Lord Overberry laughed aloud. "Poor Sir Kirby. How disappointing. When did you learn of it?"

"On one of my visits to Sarne Abbey—I forget which one—Gabriel's mother gave me a book of poetry with the sonnet in it. I made enquiries and learned the whole story. I checked every detail. I went to see the cave myself. Clotilde Edrington and I went through it together. It was delightful to look at, but quite worthless."

Lord Overberry chuckled.

"I am glad to see you retain your sense of humour. I wonder if Sir Kirby Hookmeadow will."

"You mean to tell him?"

"Certainly. The very next time I see him."

"You may do so today if you wish. He is here, in the dining room. And now, if you will excuse me, I really must find Zoë...."

BELLE WAS IN THE HALL, drawing on a pair of white kid gloves when Nona Fitzjames emerged from the library.

"So," declared Nona Fitzjames, "you thought you could get away with it!"

Bellemaine gazed in astonishment at her former ally. "I beg your pardon?"

"You deceived me! You deceived Gabriel! You deceived the entire county!"

Bellemaine laughed nervously. "Wh-what do you mean?"

"Did you think I would not discover your fraud? Admiral Anstruther, indeed! Born in Saint James's Palace, indeed!"

Bellemaine went pale. "I—I—"

"How dare you! How dare you mock me! How dare you aspire to marry Gabriel! How dare you presume to call yourself a lady! You deserve to be pilloried! Publicly chastised!"

Bellemaine stared at her in horror. The colour drained from her face. She sank into a dead faint.

CHAPTER NINETEEN

"I THINK YOU HAD BEST carry Miss Anstruther into the library," said Nona Fitzjames crisply.

Sir Kirby Hookmeadow obliged. "It is fortunate I was coming out of the dining room at that moment, is it not, Miss Fitzjames?" He lowered Bellemaine's lifeless form into an armchair and began chafing her wrists.

"Some might consider it so."

Sir Kirby Hookmeadow glanced up, puzzled by the coldness in her tone. "I don't follow you."

Nona Fitzjames sniffed. "The sooner Miss Anstruther recovers, the sooner she can depart. The sooner she departs, the better. The same goes for you."

"Madam?"

"I know everything." Her tone was authoritative and carried conviction.

Sir Kirby Hookmeadow blenched. "Everything?" His voice quavered.

"Your delusion about the diamond mine is laughable."

"Delusion?" Sir Kirby gulped.

"The diamond mine was a mere figure of speech in a sonnet by one of the Edringtons. It referred to a cave with strange formations which sparkled in the lantern light like jewels. You can see it for yourself as you leave!''

Sir Kirby Hookmeadow turned a peculiar shade of green.

''And as for Bellemaine Anstruther,'' continued Nona Fitzjames with relish, ''her antecedents are such that if I were her, I would be ashamed to show my face in society.''

Sir Kirby Hookmeadow stared.

''Knowing what I know,'' Nona Fitzjames went on relentlessly, ''about the pair of you, I can see how you came to concoct that ridiculous story about Mr. and Mrs. Edrington not being married. How base! How vile! How despicable!''

Bellemaine groaned.

''She is coming round,'' said Sir Kirby.

''Excellent. When she does, you can remove her, since you seem to have taken charge of her.'' Nona Fitzjames was frosty and unyielding. ''I take no leave of you.'' She swept toward the door.

''Er, one moment, Miss Fitzjames!'' called Sir Kirby.

''Yes?''

''These, er, revelations...''

Nona Fitzjames pursed her lips. ''Yes?''

''There is no need for everyone to know, is there?''

Nona Fitzjames drew herself up. She looked down on Sir Kirby and Bellemaine from a superior height. ''Your fate is in your own hands. I assure you that no lady and no gentleman would demean themselves by gossiping about your unfortunate positions. How-

'ever, if we learn that you have been slandering the future Countess of Sarne, or the present Earl, it will be another matter! Then the whole of England will learn of your folly and your shame!"

THE DRAWING ROOM had become remarkably crowded. Everyone seemed to have found their way into it. And it was no surprise that, as Bellemaine and Sir Kirby Hookmeadow left the house, Nona Fitzjames should come in, too.

Nona related at great length the dreadful secrets which she had learned from Lord Overberry. Dramatically, she described how she had confronted Bellemaine and Sir Kirby with the "awful truth" and how she had "thrust them forth!"

Then, as she concluded, she fixed her gaze on the Bushens and took the opportunity to congratulate them on Melissa's marriage.

"A worthy son-in-law," she observed of Arthur.

Mr. and Mrs. Bushens accepted with evident pride. They had been converted to the idea of the marriage when Zoë had innocently remarked that there was no reason why Arthur should not receive a title from the Prince Regent—one day in the future.

They had begun by calculating on a knighthood, or perhaps a baronetcy, or possibly even a barony. And within five minutes they had raised Arthur to the level of a duke. A worthy son-in-law indeed!

Nona Fitzjames went on to offer her congratulations to Lucinda. She remarked that she had always liked her and that she felt sure she would make Lord Sarne very happy.

Lucinda blushed and stammered her thanks.

"Of course," Nona Fitzjames went on, "I knew the rumour about your parents not being married was quite ridiculous. They were married in . . . in . . ." She coughed. "Ahem, the name of the place escapes me."

"It escapes all of us," said Arthur gloomily.

"What do you mean?"

Fernand sighed. "Nobody can remember where they were married."

A melancholy silence fell.

"Well!" declared Zoë brightly. "They must have been married somewhere on the south coast. So all we have to do is check the registers in each parish church . . ."

"Which," concluded Arthur, with a deep and long-suffering sigh, "should only take us the next ten years."

Zoë grimaced.

Nona Fitzjames turned to Lucinda. "Well, you can't marry Gabriel until you find out. What will people say?"

Everyone looked miserable. It was then the door opened and Dominique walked in, leaning on Mr. Liggatt's arm.

"Why is everyone looking so mournful?" she asked. And then, before anyone had a chance to reply. "Fernand! What have you done to your foot?"

Fernand tried to rise. He was pushed back into his place by Arthur. "I twisted my ankle on the staircase of the Royal Oak Inn."

Dominique frowned. "And what were you doing there?"

"Fernand thought we—Arthur and I—had fled to Gretna Green," explained Melissa. "The poor man went haring north and it wasn't until he twisted his ankle that he realized that we would never go *there* to be married!"

"Oh, Fernand!" Dominique shook her head in despair. By then Mr. Liggatt had helped her across the room and eased her onto the sofa next to her husband.

"Now, tell me," urged Dominique a second time, "what ails you all? It cannot be solely poor Fernand's leg."

"The matter," answered Nona Fitzjames, "is that we cannot find out where Lucinda's parents were married. And it is a serious matter, since there have been hints that they were *not* married!"

"But that is ridiculous!" exclaimed Dominique.

"Oh, I quite agree," said Zoë. "But neither Arthur nor Fernand can tell us where they were married. Lucinda says she never knew and—"

"And why did nobody ask me?" demanded Dominique.

A great shout arose. *"You?"*

Dominique preened, pleased with the sensation she had caused. "Yes—me. I don't suppose you considered that perhaps I might know?"

"How would you know?" questioned Fernand.

"Because your dear mama told me."

There was a gasp of astonishment.

"Oh, most wonderful!" cried Lord Sarne. He had seated himself on the arm of Lucinda's chair. His hand was resting lightly, but possessively, on her shoulder.

"But why?" queried Arthur.

"Because when she was ill—in her last illness, too," replied Dominique, "she had a feeling that she should tell someone. I was there. So she told me."

"Do, please, tell us," urged Lucinda.

"Certainly. But I must do it in my own way."

"Do it any way you please!" returned Lord Sarne. "So long as we know the place."

CHAPTER TWENTY

"IT HAPPENED THUS," commenced Dominique. "Clotilde de Niverne, my mother-in-law, arrived in Dover in 1794. Penniless. Although she stayed at an inn, she could not afford to pay for it. She was afraid to seek help, afraid to give her real name. Unknown to her, at the same inn was staying Cupid."

"Cupid?" questioned Arthur blankly.

"Yes. The most unlikely Cupid anybody ever had. Your dear Uncle Cerdic."

Lucinda smothered a giggle. A glance informed her that Arthur and Fernand were also trying hard not to laugh.

Dominique eyed them balefully. "Yes, I know you find his name funny. I still do not understand why." She rearranged her shawl. "Uncle Cerdic had just returned from India. He was on his way to London to see his brother—"

"Papa was in London?" interrupted Arthur.

"Yes. He was in London. That is where you were born."

"I know *that*!"

"Of course," Dominique went on quickly. "Arthur was baptized at Saint Peter's Church here, as soon as Edgar Edrington returned to Dorset."

"Precisely," murmured Nona Fitzjames.

"Anyway, Uncle Cerdic told Edgar Edrington about this Frenchwoman, this suspicious character who did not have any money but who was nursing a small child. Edgar Edrington, recently a widower, was at his wits' end to find a wet-nurse. He realized that if Clotilde de Niverne was nursing her own child, she must have a supply of milk . . ."

". . . and could therefore take on another baby," concluded Arthur.

"Exactly. He galloped all the way to Dover, intending to offer to pay Clotilde's debts if she would nurse his son."

"But—" Nona Fitzjames was scandalized "—she was a marchioness!"

"Edgar Edrington did not know that at the time," Dominique pointed out.

"But when he saw her . . ."

"When he saw her, he realized she was not as Uncle Cerdic had intimated, a common adventuress. She was a lady. He guessed that she was a victim of the Terror."

There was a collective sigh of relief.

"Clotilde was very taken with Edgar Edrington," Dominique informed them. "His manners were impeccable and she pitied the plight of the poor little boy who had no mother."

Feeling all eyes upon him, Arthur blushed and wished himself elsewhere.

Dominique thought for a moment before she went on, "Clotilde said she would be happy to feed Arthur until a wet-nurse could be found."

"Er, she was always very good to me," Arthur acknowledged.

"Edgar Edrington, though touched by her compassion, was unwilling to make a lady do such a thing."

"Quite right!" declared Lord Overberry.

"Gradually, through talking to her, Edgar Edrington found out who she was, and her history. He understood that she had been using an assumed name because she believed Fernand's life, as well as her own, were in danger. He agreed with her. He offered her the protection of his own name so that she could bring Fernand up safely, like a gentleman, until he was of age. Then he could return to France and claim his inheritance."

There was a silence.

"You mean," the Earl of Sarne finally said, "the Marquise de Niverne and Edgar Edrington were afraid that someone would try to harm Fernand before he reached his majority?"

"Definitely. And it was not surprising. In the Revolution, they guillotined children, also."

"So they had reason to keep quiet about where they were married, and when," mused Lucinda.

"*Mais, oui!* It was for protection! All the time it was for protection!"

Arthur cleared his throat. "Well, that explains why Mama and Papa never said anything about when they were married or where. But it does not tell us what we have been asking. Where *were* they married? And when?"

"*Tiens!* Did I not say?" Dominique was enjoying herself hugely. "Clotilde found herself growing very fond of Edgar Edrington. If she married him, she would be happy. Fernand would be safe. So she accepted him."

"Yes, but—"

"Patience!" Dominique cut him short. "They decided that the best thing to do would be to marry as soon as possible. Secrecy was essential, so that word would not get back to France. Therefore they had to marry in a place where they were not well known. For the same reason, there was no question of the banns being called. They had to be married by special licence."

"Such precautions!" exclaimed Nona Fitzjames.

"That is how it happened," Dominique went on, "that they were married on November twenty-third in the chapel of Torrance House in Brighton."

All eyes were bright and shining. All lips curved into smiles.

"Wonderful!" declared the Earl of Sarne. "Now we have only to send someone to Torrance House to make a copy of the details in the register."

Dominique blinked at him. "And why would you want to do that?"

"So that we have them here, in case we have to counter any rumours..."

Dominique sighed and shook her head. "But why do you want *another* copy? Isn't the one you have good enough?"

"What do you mean, Dominique?" queried Fernand.

"I mean what I say."

"The marriage lines are here?"

"Yes."

"But they can't be!" protested Lucinda. "None of us has ever seen them."

"They were kept hidden."

"What do we do now?" demanded Lord Sarne. "Tear the house apart, brick by brick?"

"Ah, men!" Dominique was disgusted. "You look in the safe in the library."

"You mean that dusty old thing behind the bookshelves which no one has touched for years?" enquired Fernand.

"Exactement."

Arthur burst out laughing. "Of course! We should have thought of that before!"

IT WAS NO MORE than five minutes later that Arthur returned to the drawing room, waving a small piece of paper. "Here they are. Mama's and Papa's marriage lines."

The document was passed from hand to hand. It was read with exclamations of astonishment and awe.

The marriage had been witnessed not merely by the Torrance family, but by Their Royal Highnesses The Duke and Duchess of York, and, most astounding of all, by the Prince of Wales.

"Our dear Prince Regent, no less!" cried Nona Fitzjames. "Who would have thought it."

"An honour indeed!" declared Mr. Bushens. "I wonder if His Royal Highness remembers the occasion."

"There is one way to find out," said Lord Sarne. "As soon as we are married, Lucinda, you shall be presented at Court." He raised her hand to his lips. "And we shall see."

It was then Mr. Liggatt cleared his throat. "I wonder if now might be the right time, my lord..." He extended a letter.

"Who is this from?" asked Lord Sarne suspiciously.

"Miss Anstruther left it to me to give to you."

Lord Sarne slit it open and read aloud:

"My dear Gabriel,
Allow me to express my warmest felicitations upon your forthcoming marriage. I hope you will be as happy with Lucinda as I shall be with Sir Kirby Hookmeadow.

"I daresay you are surprised to hear of my engagement to Sir Kirby. But you must know it has been of long standing. Ever since his wife's death, Sir Kirby has been my admirer. And now that his period of mourning is past, we shall be married in a few days by special licence.

"After we are married, we intend to put our property up for sale. Yes! We are leaving Dorset which has been a happy home to both of us for so many years!

"We are going to the Continent. Do you understand? We are leaving England—forever, alas!

"The reason is that poor Sir Kirby's health will not survive another winter here. His cough—you must have heard it!—was dreadful last year. My anxiety for him is acute.

"We shall give you the first refusal on the properties, since they both adjoin Sarne Abbey."

"How very decent of her," drawled Arthur. "Does she give you the price they want, as well?"

"No," replied Lord Sarne. "She remarks that I must consult her lawyers for that."

Arthur emitted a strange, hostile noise, something between a snort and a growl. Lord Sarne continued to read:

"I daresay you will have heard some very unkind stories about myself and Sir Kirby. Lord Overberry and Nona Fitzjames brought them to our attention. Naturally, they were most perturbed, and so were we.

"I shall not insult you by repeating such cruel and baseless accusations! I shall merely say that

I hope you will do everything in your power to refute them!

"Finally, let me say how delighted I am to hear that the rumour concerning Miss Edrington is utterly without foundation.

"Nothing has given Sir Kirby and myself greater pleasure. We shall be at great pains to ensure that anyone who mentions it to us is acquainted with the truth.

Your humble and devoted admirer and friend,
                    Bellemaine Anstruther."

"Well!" exclaimed Nona Fitzjames. "What do you make of that?"

Lord Sarne folded the letter. A quizzical expression crossed his face. "I think Belle is trying to say that if we don't spread stories about her and about Sir Kirby, they will not spread rumours about Lucinda."

Fernand snarled, "I would like to give them both a piece of my mind."

"A waste of time," commented Nona Fitzjames.

"But what are you going to do, Gabriel?" Fernand persisted. "How can you answer such a letter?"

"I shall answer it very simply," said Lord Sarne, "by thanking Belle for her congratulations, telling her the details of your parents' marriage so she can't deny them later, and saying I have no intention of encouraging anyone to spread cruel or baseless accusations about either herself or Sir Kirby."

Fernand was still scowling. "Belle and Sir Kirby have upset all of us. I don't see that they should escape scot-free!"

"Scot-free?" said Lucinda. "Poor Belle is to be married to Sir Kirby. What a fate!"

"Scot-free?" teased Arthur. "Poor Sir Kirby is to be married to Belle. What a penance!"

There was general laughter.

"You need not fear that Belle and Sir Kirby will get away with anything," commented Lord Overberry. "By exiling themselves, they have chosen a far harsher punishment than anything we might have imposed."

Dominique smiled. "You must not imagine, Vincent, that because you do not live on the Continent, it is a miserable place, filled only with poor, sad wretches!"

Lord Overberry returned her smile. "I didn't think that for a moment. But—" he hesitated, then turned to Lord Sarne "—do you remember Lord Byron in Italy, Gabriel?"

The earl nodded. "He was so terribly lonely, and so very unhappy. He seized hold of each British visitor with the eagerness of a dying man in the desert grasping one last glass of water. It was pitiful."

"And do you think this is how Belle and Sir Kirby will feel?" asked Melissa.

"Eventually, yes," stated Lord Overberry. "Their reputations will follow them, you see. And while they can change their residence, they cannot change their characters. Continental society will shun them when it learns the truth about them. Just as we would shun them, if they had remained here."

"But if we don't tell," protested Fernand, "how—?"

"We are not the only ones who know about them," observed Lord Sarne. "Besides, their sudden departure will set tongues wagging. And gossip has a way of...spreading."

There was a short silence.

Then Nona Fitzjames had the last word. "I believe that we can be agreed that when they marry, Belle and Sir Kirby will create their own private hell. For two more ill-suited people I have seldom come across."

LUCINDA WORE a white silk gown for her presentation to the Prince Regent. Jewels glittered at her neck and wrists. White plumes swayed with each nod of her head.

She floated across the light blue carpet of Carlton House's Crimson Drawing Room. She marvelled at the crystal chandeliers, the sumptuous furnishings and the crimson satin brocade draperies, heavily fringed with gold.

Rubens's *Landscape with Saint George* caught her eye. The *Jewish Bride*, said to be by Rembrandt, also made her want to stop and stare. Other paintings slipped by in a blur.

The Prince Regent was standing by the black marble fireplace at the far end of the room. He wore a rich dark blue velvet coat, heavily embroidered with silver thread.

How imposing he is! Lucinda thought. Then she caught a mischievous twinkle in his eye. *And how kind!* she added, as she sank into a deep curtsey.

The Prince Regent's brows drew together. "You know," he remarked, "you remind me strongly of a lady whose wedding I witnessed. She was Clotilde, Marquise de Niverne. Is she any relation of yours?"

"My mother, Your Royal Highness," murmured Lucinda.

"Ah, so that's it! I thought I saw a likeness." The Prince Regent studied her for a moment, then addressed Lord Sarne. "You are a lucky man."

"Thank you, Your Royal Highness."

LUCINDA WAS RELIEVED when the presentation was over. The Prince Regent had been consideration itself, but even so, it had been an ordeal.

She compared her visit to Carlton House, bound with pomp and circumstance and etiquette, with the informality of her wedding.

Fernand, Arthur, Mrs. Bushens, Melissa, Zoë, Lord Overberry—everyone had been in favour of a sumptuous wedding.

Lord Sarne had eyed them sourly. He was not going to wait while such an affair was organized. He had, he said, waited for Lucinda long enough. He refused to wait any longer. He wanted her—now.

And Lucinda, whose mind accorded very well with his, had smiled, said nothing, and let him browbeat them into submission.

Lucinda's wedding dress had been the unadorned white muslin gown in which her mother had been married. Hebe had found it for her, packed in a trunk in the attic at Bluebell Manor. The wedding had taken place in the ancient, gilded chapel of Sarne Abbey, with its fan-vaulted ceiling and its stained-glass windows.

Afterward, Fernand had hurried Dominique home to the Château Niverne, where a lusty boy had soon seen the light of day.

It was a pity they would not be able to come to Zoë and Vincent's wedding, mused Lucinda. That was going to be in a few days' time. However, since they were now married neither Lucinda nor Melissa could be bridesmaids, as had originally been planned; this honour fell to two of Zoë's unmarried cousins. Instead, Lucinda and Melissa were to witness the details of the marriage inscribed in the Parish Register.

Lucinda handed her heavy, formal, presentation gown to Hebe, and slipped into a rose-pink negligée. The sheer silk caressed her lithe, slender body, pleasing her senses. She left the dressing room and entered the master bedroom of Lord Sarne's Town house.

He was stretched out on the bed. His black eyes followed her every movement. "I forgot to tell you—Liggatt came to see me this afternoon."

"Oh?"

"He and Hebe wish to marry."

"You gave them your blessing, I hope."

"I did." He ran his hands through his dark hair. "We must see that she has a decent dowry."

Lucinda smiled. "Yes." It would be pleasant to be able to provide well for Hebe, who had been so loyal to her!

She stood at the foot of the bed, gazing at her husband. His bronzed torso was only half-covered by his dressing gown.

Even when we first met, when he looked at me, she thought, *at that very first moment...even then, I was drawn to him...*

Lord Sarne reached out both hands toward her. "Come!"

His voice was half imperious, half pleading.

Lucinda went to him and settled herself in his arms. As she kissed him, her cinnamon curls brushed against his cheek and her negligée spread across him.

"I love you, Gabriel."

"And I love you, Lucinda." His voice had become husky with desire. "You'll never know how much...."

Harlequin Regency Romance™

COMING NEXT MONTH

#21 LESSONS FOR A LADY by Barbara Neil
When Susanna Marlowe's father must flee the
country, the scandal reduces her to penury and social
disgrace. Edward Farrineau, her childhood friend,
arranges her circumstances so that she will not starve.
Susanna loves Edward, but she knows she is too wild,
outspoken and unrefined for him. It comes as no
surprise when Edward announces his betrothal to a
lady of genteel birth. But when Edward is enlisted to
help find Susanna a suitable match, he is strangely
reluctant. Encouraged by his reaction, Susanna
undertakes lessons on becoming a lady with surprising
and often hilarious results.

#22 SPANISH COIN by Margaret Westhaven
Mary Winter and her disabled father are rescued at
Holland House by a tall, dark and handsome stranger.
The next time they meet is when they are taking their
vows. Count Antonio Ramirez y Mondego of Castile
seemed oddly eager to make Mary his bride and her
father, Captain Winter, nearly has apoplexy when he
learns of the marriage. He warns Mary to guard her
garnet necklace, the only heirloom her mother, a
Spanish Countess, bequeathed to her. When the
necklace disappears Mary confronts Antonio with the
theft. He insists she is sadly mistaken. A quick trip to
a London bank and an antique treasure chest reveal
that Antonio had been a hero all along and now he
truly belonged to her.

February brings you ...

PENNY JORDAN

valentine's night

Sorrel didn't particularly want to meet her long-lost cousin Val from Australia. However, since the girl had come all this way just to make contact, it seemed a little churlish not to welcome her.

As there was no room at home, it was agreed that Sorrel and Val would share the Welsh farmhouse that was being renovated for Sorrel's brother and his wife. Conditions were a bit primitive, but that didn't matter.

At least, not until Sorrel found herself snowed in with the long-lost cousin, who turned out to be a handsome, six-foot male!

Also, look for the next Harlequin Presents Award of Excellence title in April:

Elusive as the Unicorn
by Carole Mortimer

HP1243-1

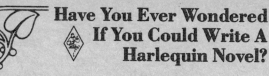

Have You Ever Wondered If You Could Write A Harlequin Novel?

Here's great news—Harlequin is offering a series of cassette tapes to help you do just that. Written by Harlequin editors, these tapes give practical advice on how to make your characters—and your story—come alive. There's a tape for each contemporary romance series Harlequin publishes.

Mail order only

All sales final

HARLEQUIN
American Romance®

Join in the

Rocky Mountain Magic

Experience the charm and magic of The Stanley Hotel in the Colorado Rockies with #329 BEST WISHES this month, and don't miss out on further adventures to take place there in the next two months.

In March 1990 look for #333 SIGHT UNSEEN by Kathy Clark and find out what psychic visions lie ahead for Hayley Austin's friend Nicki Chandler. In April 1990 read #337 RETURN TO SUMMER by Emma Merritt and travel back in time with their friend Kate Douglas.

ROCKY MOUNTAIN MAGIC—All it takes is an open heart. Only from Harlequin American Romance

All the Rocky Mountain Magic Romances take place at the beautiful Stanley Hotel.

Harlequin Superromance®

LET THE GOOD TIMES ROLL...

Add some Cajun spice to liven up your New Year's celebrations and join Superromance for a romantic tour of the rich Acadian marshlands and the legendary Louisiana bayous.

Starting in January 1990, we're launching CAJUN MELODIES, a three-book tribute to the fun-loving people who've enriched America by introducing us to crawfish étouffé and gumbo, zydeco music and the Saturday night party, the *fais-dodo*. And learn about loving, Cajun-style, as you meet the tall, dark, handsome men who win their ladies' hearts with a beautiful, haunting melody....

Book One: *Julianne's Song*, January 1990
Book Two: *Catherine's Song*, February 1990
Book Three: *Jessica's Song*, March 1990